Scary Shorts
For
Halloween

A collection of true ghost stories

Edited by
Janet Sanger

Published by Accent Press Ltd – 2004
IBSN 0954489942
Copyright © The Authors 2004

Printed and bound in UK
By Clays Plc, St Ives.

Cover Design by Richie Perrott
Desert Point Illustration.
www.desertpointillustration.com

This book is dedicated to those striving to find a cure for breast cancer and the fundraisers who support them.

Special thanks to the authors for generously donating their stories.

Acknowledgement

'A Logical Experience' by Della Galton was originally published in Woman's Weekly Fiction Special in 2001.

Contents

The Hampton Court Ghost

Gone are the days of ghost stories being confined to ancient myths told around camp fires. The phenomenon of souls lost somewhere between this world and the next is a very hot topic. Entire TV channels are dedicated to the research and exposure of the paranormal. Modern technology has added to the certainty that ghosts are fact not fiction – as seen in this CCTV picture of the Hampton Court Ghost.

My Ghosts
By Yvette Fielding

I have been asked many questions throughout my career in television and one of the most significant is; why did I decide to become a ghost hunter? It's a fair question which raises many eyebrows when I confide my reason. Five years ago my husband, Karl and our son William moved into a little cottage in Cheshire. I was pregnant at the time with our daughter Mary, so I was very keen to move in as soon as possible. I felt it was everything we wanted in a property and I had fallen in love with it as soon as I'd seen it. My husband, on the other hand, wasn't as keen but could see how taken I was and so signed the papers.

The first year at the cottage went very quickly and both William and I were very happy. Karl on the other hand seemed withdrawn and told me that he felt uncomfortable in the house, almost as if he wasn't welcome. Every morning he would wake up with bad headaches, followed by feelings of depression.

I couldn't understand why Karl was feeling this way and was a little upset that he was feeling so low in our new cottage. When he went to work he returned to his normal fun self. When we went out

1

for the evening or went for walks with the children his mood was jovial and carefree, but every time we returned home it was almost as if a big black cloud had descended over him.

When our daughter Mary was born, it seemed the cloud had lifted, and Karl felt on top of the world. Everyone was happy and our lives were now complete. Little did we know life in our little cottage was about to change dramatically…

Strange things started to happen when Mary was about six months old. I noticed that she would smile and laugh as if something or someone had just walked into the room. At first I thought nothing of it until both Karl and I heard William, who was six at the time, talking to someone in his room late one night. We presumed it was William talking in his sleep, but things became clear when our little boy told us that a lady in a white dress came and talked to him late at night. In fact both Karl and I had become so concerned that we set up a nightly vigil to try and find out exactly what, if anything, was keeping them awake.

We were amazed to hear our children, who were sleeping in different rooms, chattering away and laughing as if they were both engaged in conversation with someone. We opened the door only to discover there was no one there and the children were fast asleep.

A few weeks later Karl had to go and work in London for a few days. I was a little apprehensive at being in the house on my own as I had become edgy and nervous after hearing the children's strange chatter. My imagination was working overtime. Did we have a ghost in the house? If we did, it obviously wasn't a bad spirit as it seemed to love the children.

On the night that Karl had gone to London I had put the children to bed and was sitting downstairs watching some television. My viewing was interrupted by a loud buzzing sound. I sat bolt upright and turned the TV down. The noise was coming from the kitchen. I ventured slowly towards the door and turned the handle cautiously. I remember hearing another sound, a deep pounding noise. I realised it was my heart. I was petrified!

I opened the door slowly and discovered that all the lights in the kitchen were turning on and off. They buzzed and flickered repeatedly. I knew there had to be some sort of electrical fault but it didn't make me feel any better. Why had this not happened before? I knew it wasn't a problem with the bulbs as I had recently replaced them. I turned the switch off, closed the door and walked out. I sat back down again and after a short while began to feel a little better. I told myself off for being so stupid and nervous, ghosts indeed!

Five minutes later I got the shock of my life. The noise was deafening! It was as if all the cupboard doors were being slammed shut one after the other. I sat upright and motionless, fear ran through every vein in my body. My hands shook and my stomach lurched repeatedly as though I was on a roller coaster ride. Was someone in my house? Was there really a ghost in my home?

I went nervously into the kitchen. Nothing was out of place; the cupboard doors were closed and the lights were… on?! I distinctly remember turning them off! Enough was enough; I decided to call it a night and go to bed (with the lights on!).

Once tucked up in bed with a good book I started to feel a little better. Logic had kicked in and I had just about convinced myself that what had just happened downstairs was all in my mind. I had been working hard of late and Mary had us up in the middle of the night with teething problems. However, my logic was about to fly out of the window and my early night was going to be a long one!

As I sat there beginning to relax, I heard another noise coming from the landing. Karl and I had fitted a safety gate at the top of the staircase so Mary would not fall down the stairs. It took a lot of strength and effort to undo the gate, so you can imagine my horror as I heard the gate pop open and heard the sound of it creaking, as if someone was opening it.

There couldn't be someone in the house...could there?! I froze, I couldn't move and I couldn't scream as I didn't want to alarm the children. I plucked up the courage to scramble out of bed and walked towards the landing. Every inch of my body was covered in sweat, and tears were rolling down my cheeks. Never have I been so terrified in my life! If there was a burglar in my house, I had to protect the children.

When I saw the safety gate closed and to my relief found no one in the house, I ran to the phone. I could not and would not put up with a ghost in my house. Forget rational, forget logic, this was not my imagination, and I did not want to witness any more strange ghostly goings on in my home. Fortunately Karl hadn't reached Birmingham yet and when he heard my uncontrollable sobs over the phone, he came straight back.

That night marked the start of a period of regular activity; doors banging, light bulbs blowing, and the telephone ringing when no one was there. The television had also developed a mind of its own by switching itself on and off. Sometimes we'd go to switch it back on and realise that it hadn't even been plugged in! More disturbingly were the noises coming from the kitchen as if furniture was being dragged around.

One particular night I was just drifting off to sleep and Karl was watching television downstairs. I turned on to my side and there lying next to me on the bed was an old woman! Well I couldn't contain myself and screamed the bloody place down! After Karl had told the children that mummy had just had a nightmare, they went back to bed. He then had the job of trying to calm me down and convince me that I had been dreaming – he didn't have much luck!

We couldn't stand it any more and so called in a psychic. Karl and I didn't know what to expect. I think we both imagined some strange, small person to appear on our doorstep similar to the psychic in the film "Poltergeist". Mark was a very ordinary, pleasant man who put us at ease straight away. He walked around the house on his own and then sat us down and told us of the lady who used to live in our house, and as it turned out didn't want to leave.

According to Mark, an elderly woman once lived here in the late 1600's with her husband and

5

daughter. This woman was treated badly by her husband, who liked to drink a lot. One day the house caught fire and the woman and her daughter were killed. The room they died in was our bedroom.

Mark mentioned that when he went into our room he could see smoke and sensed a feeling of sadness. He then asked if either of us was experiencing headaches or depression. When Karl told Mark how he had been feeling since the day he had moved in, Mark explained this was the reason. He also explained that this woman did not like men but found children a delight. It was all fitting together but why all the noises? Why create such a commotion that we were now terrified to live in our own home? According to Mark, it was her way of attracting attention.

Before Mark left, he asked to be left alone in the house, where he then performed an exorcism. This didn't take long and when the job was complete, we were full of gratitude and optimism. As soon as Mark left it seemed as if a dark cloud had been lifted from the house and our lives returned to normal. Karl's headaches disappeared along with the depression, and our fairy tale cottage became a reality.

Some months later we decided to lift the flag stones up in the back garden to replace them with a lawn for the children to play on. It wasn't long before the stones had all gone and just as the workmen were finishing off, they discovered something buried beneath the ground. They unearthed what appeared to be mysterious glass and pot jugs. We later asked an expert to look at the items, he dated them from the 1600's and confirmed that they would probably have been used to hold alcohol. I was intrigued and fascinated by this information. Could these bottles and jars have once belonged to the lady's husband? And did he bury them in the garden?

In fact, despite feeling terrified at the time, the whole episode has proved to be very influential. To date, I have now visited and investigated over ninety reputedly haunted locations in Great Britain and Europe. Along the way, I have gained greater knowledge, a better understanding, and a little courage. I will keep going until I discover the truth about ghosts, until then, sleep tight!

Descent Into Chaos
By Anne Caulfield

Tricia folded her arms and slouched back into the chair. 'I'm here now, so why don't you give it a try?', she asked.

'Everything is flat my dear,' said Mrs. Robinson gently. 'I can't give you clairvoyance if Spirit doesn't want to make contact.'

In that case, I'd better have the Tarot cards instead.' She nodded at the pack still wrapped up on the table.

The medium hesitated for a moment before reaching for her cards. 'I'll try one last time,' she said, as she removed the purple silk material which covered them. 'But as I've told you before, you should stop going from one psychic to another. It's not healthy to keep delving into the occult in this way.'

Tricia watched her as she mixed the cards. 'What I get up to when I leave your home has nothing to do with you. It's not as though I don't pay you.'
The medium passed the cards across the table and sighed. 'Give them a good shuffle and cut them twice with your left hand.'

Tricia did as she was asked and passed them back.

9

As she laid them out in front of her, Mrs Robinson said, 'It's up to you if you want to waste your money being told the same thing over and over again.'

Tricia watched as each card was placed into position. Although she'd never studied the Tarot she remembered the meanings of some of them. The Tower and The Devil, sitting in front of her now, were the most familiar.

I see I've got the usual two next to each other,' she said.

Well the warning is still there. Look at this spread' The medium tapped several cards with her forefinger. 'These alone signify a mental breakdown.' She laid the last one. 'The card of Death with the others in these positions...' She shook her head and began to gather them up.

'Aren't you going to carry on?'

No,' said the medium, as she pushed herself away from the table. 'There's too much darkness around you. You're wasting my time anyway, because you never listen to what I say.' She crossed the room and opened the door. 'I wish you luck though, because you're going to need it.'

Tricia turned to the last but one page in the local paper. She'd been to all of the clairvoyants, psychics and mediums advertised here. They all knew her quite well too, just like that stupid old bat, Robinson. At least two of them had warned her off before now. No point in seeing them again.

She was about to throw the paper down, when a boxed advert at the bottom of the page caught her eye.

"Robin Price will demonstrate clairvoyance on Thursday, 12th February, at Stoneleigh Spiritualist Church. Doors open at 7pm. All are welcome."

Robin Price, Tricia thought, I haven't heard of him before. Worth a try, I suppose. She decided to check him out.

Robin Price looked out over the congregation and saw there were more empty chairs than full ones. He didn't mind too much. A good grounding was essential to a medium. Stoneleigh was a small town, with only one Spiritualist Church, and the Booking Secretary sounded quite pleased when he offered his services. Doubtful if any of the big-wigs come out here to demonstrate, he thought, as his gaze drifted over the mainly elderly women seated before him.

He felt the pull of someone's aura, and turned his head in that direction. It was a young woman of about twenty five, sitting in the front row gazing up at him.

So many people did this. Willing you to go to them. A reading could be messed up that way. He'd been taught to go where his guides instructed and no amount of will-power from this young lady would change his mind.

Turning away from her, he closed his eyes and waited for the voice of his guide to direct him. A familiar chill enveloped him as his spirit guide drew close, followed by a light pressure at the base of his right ear. Drawing his psychic energy through

11

his body, he listened for the voice of his spirit mentor.

'Sykes. Tricia Sykes.' He heard the name clearly in his mind.

'I want someone with the surname of Sykes,' he called out.

Two people put up their hands. One elderly. The other was the young woman.

Unlikely to be the old girl, he thought, with a name like Tricia. But I'd better ask.

'I'm looking for Tricia Sykes,' he said, looking at the elderly lady. She shook her head and shouted, 'Sorry, thought you said, Pikes.'

'My name is Tricia.' The young girl, in her excitement, had left her seat and now stood in front of him.

'Alright love,' he said, 'go back to your seat and try to relax. It helps to make my mediumship stronger if you're calm.' He waited whilst she settled herself, before continuing.

'Although you're aware that you're psychic, you haven't developed your ability yet, have you?'

She shook her head.

'Let me hear your voice?' he asked. 'It makes the communication stronger.'

'Oh. Okay then.' She hesitated and then called out again. 'I have been trying to do something about it.'

'So I'm being told. But you mustn't dabble.' He listened again to his guide. 'You're going about it the wrong way my love. It's dangerous to mess around with a Ouija board, because you won't have

12

protection, and it's a sure way of inviting unwanted entities into your aura.'

'I haven't been messing around with anything.' The girl sounded defiant as she looked around her. The congregation was silent, and many had their heads turned in her direction.

Robin checked with his guide to see if he'd heard correctly. 'I can only repeat the message my spirit guide is telling me. You must learn how to close your psychic centres because at the moment you're like a bright beacon on the darker surface of the lower astral plane.'

'Well I have been studying a book on this subject and following its advice,' Tricia said.

'Don't believe everything you read,' he answered. 'It's important that you join a proper circle, with a good medium in charge. In the early stages you need protection, plus feed-back from other students. How will you know if it's Spirit communicating otherwise?'

Tricia shrugged her shoulders and didn't answer. 'You've been told this several times before, haven't you?'

She folded her arms and looked away. Obviously thinks she knows it all, Robin thought. Seeing he wasn't going to get any further, he cleared his aura and waited to be guided to someone else.

Tricia sat at the table in the spare bedroom she used as an office. It was quite dark, for the evening was drawing in, and she had pulled the curtains across. The only illumination came from a candle alight in front of her.

She shifted the candle a little closer to the note pad, aware that there was just enough light to jot down notes.

She looked around the room. On the desk she'd placed a large wooden cross, with a huge chunk of obsidian in front of it. The cross was for protection, and the crystal to clear the air of negativity. The book stated that they would help.

On the wall was a poster of Sai Baba. Probably one of Jesus would have been better, but the Indian guru was the only one she could find. Still, he was a famous avatar in India, therefore his picture should add to the protection.

The candle sent flickering shadows into the corners, and once or twice she could have sworn there was other movement, but she put it down to her imagination.

She was probably a bit unsettled by all of the readings she'd had. Thinking they all knew best, just because they were older than her. Times had changed, and she had no intention of spending months on end developing her psychic ability. Leaning forward, she placed her elbows on the desk, and her head in her hands. Breathing deeply, she closed her eyes and visualised white light rising through her body. She could feel it physically, and was sexually aroused as the energy swarmed around her hips and between her thighs.

She knew she had to get the energy higher, so she concentrated hard on the white light. Her stomach gave a lurch, followed by a pain in her throat and in the centre of her forehead. It was a few moments before she was aware of the

14

cold. Her feet were like ice. Reaching behind her, she felt the radiator. It was hot.

She stood up and went in search of a pair of socks. Finding an old pair in the corner of a drawer, she quickly pulled them on. She was aware of how much warmer it was in the bedroom in comparison to the spare room. She thought it could be to do with the way the house was built.

She settled back into the office chair, and went over the energy exercise again. This time she found it reached the top of her head far more quickly than before.

But she still couldn't get warm. At this rate she would lose concentration. She was about to get up again, when a guttural voice quite clearly called her name, 'Tricia.' Not daring to move, she held her breath, and stared into the gloom to where she thought the voice had come from. She could have sworn there was movement within the shadows thrown by the candle. There seemed to be a vague outline of a figure. She blinked. It was still there and becoming more substantial. The figure was hooded, with its head down so she couldn't see the face.

Was this a guide, she asked herself? Yes, of course it was. But why did she feel nervous? Guides aren't supposed to make you scared.

Then his rasping voice came again. 'Tricia,' and she was sure the figure beckoned her. The coldness was bitter, seeping over her feet and twisting around her legs. Her breath was a misty outline hovering in front of her face. And then, the candle went out. Terrified, she stumbled towards the door. She heard the flapping of wings and something grazed her face.

She yanked at the handle and the door flew open, crashing against the wall. Groping for the light switch, she heaved with relief as the landing flooded with brightness. It wasn't until she reached the kitchen that she'd stopped running. Looking back she saw nothing. She'd flicked on every light she'd passed, and no shadows hugged the walls. Fighting to get her panic under control, she leaned with her back against the sink, unable to take her gaze away from the empty hall in front of her. The only sound she could hear was the clicking of the radiator.

It took her a few minutes to get her breathing into an even rhythm, but by then she knew she had to go back to check out the room. As quietly as she could, she made her way upstairs on the balls of her feet, ready for flight. Although she listened, it was difficult to hear anything other than the pounding of her heart.

Hesitating on the last step, she cautiously turned her head, looking towards the spare room. The door was still open and she could see part-way into the room. Everything was silent and appeared to be normal. Stepping onto the landing she peered further into her office, watching for the slightest movement. With the light on, she could see there were no wriggling phantoms anywhere. Taking a deep breath she ventured through the door. The coldness had gone and the room was quite warm, although it smelt a bit musty. She looked into the corner where she'd seen the figure. Nothing. Thank God. It must have been her imagination.

She opened the window a little to dispel the stale air. With a final look around, she closed the door behind her.

When she returned to the kitchen she made a mug of coffee and at last, began to unwind a little. There was no doubt that she'd had one hell of a scare.

'Bloody-well serves me right.' She said out loud. 'I've been told enough times not to mess about with it. And now look what's happened.' She carried her coffee from the kitchen, along the hall and into the living room. Still shivering, she lit the gas fire. Standing in front of it, she stared into the flames as she sipped from the mug. She told herself she had to find a class or a circle. She wasn't going to sit alone again, that's for sure.

Leaning down, she turned the fire up a bit more. It seemed to be taking longer than usual to heat the room. She straightened, picked up the empty mug, and turned towards the door. Suspended in the air across the centre of the room, were several faces. Her mouth opened but the scream caught in her throat. Transfixed with horror, she saw that the faces appeared to be made of a white, misty substance. Each one was contorted, as though they were looking into the face of Hell itself.

'Oh God, no,' she whimpered. 'What have I done?'

As she spoke the faces began to disperse. Moments later, only a small tendril remained which then drifted towards the wall before disappearing. She collapsed onto the couch and tried to control her trembling limbs. A few minutes later, after several

17

deep breaths, she made her way back to the kitchen. Fishing out the telephone book, she looked up the number for The College of Psychic Studies. She knew she had to get help.

After explaining what had happened, she expected the woman to tell her how stupid she'd been. But she didn't. Instead, she was sympathetic.

'There isn't much we can do for you tonight Tricia, but we can have someone out to your house tomorrow morning who will cleanse away any negative energy that has built up.'

'But what shall I do about tonight?' She was still agitated. 'I'm too scared to go to bed.'

'As your office is back to normal, I think everything will be all right. You saw faces in the living room because you were still giving off negative energy.

'Go back in there and see if the temperature's back to normal. I'll hold on while you do it.'

Tricia put down the phone, walked along the hall and peered through the doorway.

'Everything seems okay,' she said when she returned.

'In that case, I suggest you try to stop thinking about your experience. It's important to let it go. Watching television will take your mind off of it.'

'Isn't there anything else I can do to protect myself? I placed a wooden cross and a crystal in my room, but it obviously wasn't enough.'

'I'm afraid physical objects won't have any effect,' the woman said. 'You're working with non-physical beings, so the best form of defence is your mind. You'll learn how to do this if you join a circle.

18

For now though, try to visualise yourself inside a glass container. Do this each time your thoughts wander back to what happened. It will help to strengthen your mind.' She then added, 'Now try not to worry dear. We'll have someone at your address first thing in the morning.'

Tricia reluctantly replaced the phone. It felt like her only link to safety. My God, how she needed a drink. Taking out a tumbler along with the whisky bottle, she poured amber liquid half way up the glass, and then carried both through to the living room. She picked up the remote and skipped from channel to channel, stopping at some award ceremony for minor celebrities. It wasn't riveting enough for her to forget earlier events, but as time wore on and the whisky diminished, so she became more relaxed. From the first commercial break, she concentrated her mind on the glass cage. At first it seemed to work, but by the time the programme had ended along with the booze, there was no way she could visualise anything. She knew she was drunk, but it was helping her to forget things. All she wanted now was her bed.

Switching off the television, she made her way upstairs. Although wobbly and light-headed, she was still aware of feeling uneasy, as though someone was walking behind her. It wasn't surprising that she felt this way after everything that had happened. Once in bed, she reached out and switched off the lamp, and then burrowed down under the duvet to get warm.

Moments later, as she was drifting off to sleep, her bed was lifted violently into the air before being dropped with a loud thwack back onto the floor. She yelled as she fell out onto the carpet. In her panic she scrabbled on all fours before standing and feeling for the light switch. The room flooded with light, but shaking uncontrollably she held on to the door to steady herself. She saw that her bed was several feet away from the wall, and was now in a different position. Although her head was still fogged from the whisky, Tricia knew she had to get out of the house. She pulled the duvet from the bed, and leaving the lights on, weaved her way downstairs. She passed the living room, and headed down the hall. After wrapping the duvet around her shoulders, she fumbled with the key, as she tried to unlock the front door. And then she dropped it. It landed somewhere among the shoes and bags left on the floor, and she couldn't find it. She sank down and huddled in the corner, sobbing, her knees drawn up to her chest. Her eyes staring from a face filled with tension and fear.

A little after ten o'clock the following day, John and David from the College called. Although it was a cold, clear morning, they could see the glow of lights from an upstairs room and through the glass panel at the top of the front door. John rang the bell several times which brought no response from inside the house. Then he used his hand to rap on the glass. After several minutes, he bent down and looked through the letter box. He could see a young woman wrapped in a duvet, sitting on the floor. She was rocking back and forth, muttering loudly to herself.

He straightened and turned to David. 'Take a look,' he said. 'We've got a bad situation here. This girl is going to need an ambulance.'

He listened as David shouted through the letter box, 'Tricia love, can you get up and open the door for us. We're here to help you, but you've got to let us in.' A moment later he stood up and shook his head.

John used his mobile phone to call for an ambulance, and watched as David crashed again and again against the door with his shoulder. The crack was loud as the door splintered and the lock gave way. There was still no reaction from Tricia, who continued to rock back and forth. Her unblinking eyes were stark against the white of her face as she watched the stairs. John gently pulled apart her clenched hands, rubbing them to improve her circulation. Her fear was palpable. She was still talking to herself but he couldn't make sense of the words.

'Can you make out what she's trying to say David?', he asked.

'I think it's something about a bat called Robinson.' He leaned closer to Tricia. 'And a tower and the Devil.' He listened again. 'She keeps repeating the words mad, the tower and the Devil. It's the same words over and over again.'

The Girl
By Tina Brown

It was that time in the evening, just a few minutes
between dusk and the dark of night. Mum was
watering the front lawn and garden. I was riding my
billycart down the slight slope from the top of our
driveway.

I screamed when I saw it. I couldn't believe what
had just happened. It had come out of nowhere.
Mum must have dropped the hose and run to me. I
think she'd thought I'd skinned my knee or had run
over my foot with the wheel of the billycart. At the
time I didn't really notice because I was sobbing and
shaking, crying incoherently about running *her* over.
I'm sure mum thought I was blubbering about an ant
or other kind of insect.

'I just ran over a little girl.' I cried loudly
because my mother didn't seem to understand what
had happened. I clung to my mother as I looked back
up the drive to where *she* had been.

'A little girl? Don't be silly sweetheart. There
was no one there. You might have seen your own
shadow.' Thinking back now, that was a silly remark
considering that by this time the last of the fading
light had disappeared into the dark of night, leaving
only the street lights' dim glow.

23

Dark shadows surrounded us and I was feeling so very very cold and confused, Mum didn't seem to realize what had just happened. 'No she was there. A little girl and I couldn't stop.' I said all this in sobbing gulps as my whole body shook uncontrollably. I clutched Mum with the fright I was suffering and tried to explain more. 'She was just staring at me Mum but she wouldn't move and I.... I ran her over. Where is she?' I looked around at all those dark shadows waiting for *her* to jump out at me.

'There was no little girl.' Mum was adamant.

'She was real Mum. I saw her. She had brown hair and she had a long dress but she had no feet.' Again I sobbed as I saw the flowing hem of the dress that swirled around mid air. 'I couldn't see her feet.' I swallowed. 'She was standing there but she had no feet, I could only see the bottom of her dress and she was sad mum. So sad.' I started to cry at the sadness I had felt from *her* ,that solemn little girl I had ridden my billycart through.

Mum was rubbing her hands up and down my arms because I was physically shaking. I had never felt so cold before. Mum supported me into the house because I was too shaky on my legs. Wanting to go straight to the bathroom to run me a nice warm bath, Mum had to stop because I couldn't let her go. I was too scared to be away from her. So I clung to Mum while she ran the bath and when I turned and looked in the mirror I saw how pale my face was. Almost as pale as *hers,* and I could see myself still shaking uncontrollably against Mum's warm body.

24

After a few calming minutes as the comforting steam of the bath water wafted through the room I sniffled and thought aloud. 'We better go and check to make sure she's alright mum.'

'Did she cry out when you ran her over?' Mum asked.

'No I just went straight through her and she disappeared.' I shivered at the memory 'How did she do that?' I just couldn't understand it.

'She could have been a spirit or ghost come to play with you. Maybe it looked like you were having so much fun on your billycart that she wanted to join you.'

'But who is she mum?'

'I don't know sweetheart. She might be your guardian angel. She might have been a little girl that lived in an old house around here a long time ago.'

'You mean a ghost! But ghosts aren't real.' Or were they? I had thought. I had seen *her* and *she* had disappeared as quickly as *she* had appeared.

'Some people think they are.' Mum continued.

'Do you?' I asked.

'I believe that our spirits do live on.'

'Does that mean she'll come back and get me tonight.' A sudden thought of being in my room, alone, in the dark if *she* appeared scared me almost witless. *She* was going to come back and get me tonight for running her over. I was sure of it and started to cry again.

'She's not going to get you. I think she just wanted to play and when she saw that you were scared of her she disappeared.'

25

'She might be cranky with me and come back and get me when I'm asleep tonight.' I sobbed, not able to overcome the dread of *her* coming back.

'I don't think she'll do that sweetheart. I'll keep checking on you to make sure you're alright and you only have to call and I'll come running.'

It took sometime for mum to calm me down and reassure that everything was alright and that I hadn't hurt the little girl I had seen. I finally went to sleep, thoughts about the little girl I had run over with my billycart floated through my dreams.

Kirsty had finally calmed down and was asleep soundly and peacefully and her mother breathed a sigh of relief and went to relax in front of the TV. A shadowy movement caught the corner of her eye, and she turned her head quickly in the direction of the movement.

There was a wall between the front door and the living room, making a slight alcove and it was into this that the small shadowy figure had run. A shadowy figure the same size as Kirsty.

Kirsty's name was growled by her mother, because she thought Kirsty was playing her 'I can't sleep games'. In reply there was a muffled giggle.

Another growl of Kirsty's name as her mother stomped towards the alcove, hoping to scare her daughter into a 'run back to bed,' but once she rounded the wall there was no-one there. A cold chill filled the air and ran over her skin.

Kirsty's mother stopped and listened, then shivered. All was quiet. There was no way that anyone could have gotten away from that alcove without her seeing them. How the hell had Kirsty done it? Her mother scratched her head in wonder.

Marching down the hallway towards Kirsty's room, her mum was thinking how strange it was that she hadn't heard Kirsty run back to her room, or even see her leave the alcove.

Kirsty was curled up in bed sound asleep just as her mother had left her.

She wondered if she had imagined that running shadow and that muffled giggle. Couldn't it have been the same little girl Kirsty had seen earlier? Kirsty's mum thought about this all night. It was hard for her to sleep that night with the thought of a ghost in the house, even if it was a playful mischievous little girl. It was all very unnerving.

A couple of nights later Kirsty's mum was awoken by what she thought was Kirsty coming into her room complaining of not being able to sleep. With eyes closed she reached out her arm to place around Kirsty and hug her, to draw her into bed for comfort but there was nothing there but cold air. Now eyes wide open, there fading from her sight was the little girl Kirsty had described.

With a gasp Kirsty's mum turned on the bedside light. She was shaking and shivering from the experience. She wondered if it had been the tail-end of her dream but much as she tried she couldn't even remember what she had been dreaming about

.Blue Bell Hill
By Nina Tucknott

Jack woke up drenched in sweat. Again.

His heart was thumping so loudly the sound was deafening. His chest felt so unbelievably tight. Nausea welled up. He swallowed hard.

Next to him, Susan was fast asleep, blissfully unaware of his inner turmoil. Her mouth was wide open just like the girl's mouth had been. Only one thing was different; no blood was seeping out of Susan's mouth. Not a single drop of red liquid so amazingly bright to begin with, almost luminous, and then not so luminous as it turned a darker and darker red, almost black. Also, Susan's eyes were closed not wide and staring like the girl's. All right… so that made two things…

He shivered. Slipping out of bed, he headed for the study. Somewhere, in the back of the old mahogany desk, was a half-empty packet of cigarettes. He was pretty sure of that. He hadn't smoked for months and months, not since Geoff had been diagnosed with lung cancer and the whole gang had promised to stop there and then - scout's honour and all that. And now he was going to break his promise. And hope to die.

'To hell with it!'

He had this incredible urge to fill his lungs to capacity with smoke. Steely blue smoke; so bad for you. Apparently. To inhale and inhale until every crevice was filled. Strong smoke that would make him cough and splutter. Maybe so loudly that Susan would wake up? Anything, anything at all, to take his mind off things.

But would it? Would this girl ever leave him in peace? Let him forget her staring eyes, her gaping mouth? So far, she hadn't. Somehow, Jack felt she probably wasn't going to. As always, her screams were so ear-piercing. So shrill, so loud. In fact, his ears were still ringing. And her eyes… so huge, so brown, so staring. And the blood… oh the blood…

Jack picked up the wastepaper basket and retched and retched. Again.

'So… been out with friends?' Jack turned to look at the girl next to him. She was young, about twenty, with hair hanging limp around her face, having been soaked by the heavy downpour. Her jacket and long skirt clung to a curvaceous body like a second skin.

'Yes. Had a bit of a shindig. Went on longer than expected. Missed the last bus...' Her voice was quiet and soft. She brushed the wet hair away from her face and looked at him with huge brown eyes. 'We had a pizza at Marco's and then a drink or two. It was for my hen night, you see,' she volunteered.

'Wow!' Jack kept his eyes on the road. The rain was steady but playing tricks with his headlights. He dropped his speed as he was finding it difficult to see the sides of the road. 'I guess that means congratulations are in order. When's your big day?'

'Tomorrow. Two o'clock.' She was trying to pin her hair up with a couple of hair slides she'd found in her bag.

'I wish you all the best.' Jack looked at her again and she smiled back sweetly.

'Oh thanks! How kind. Graham, that's my boyfriend, me and him... we're gonna be real happy!' She settled back in the seat and sighed contentedly.

Jack switched the fan on hoping it would help to dry her hair a bit.

'Have you known him long then? Your husband-to-be' He reached for a cigarette and lit it with one hand.

'Nearly two years now. Met him at school.'

'What a coincidence, it's the same with me and my wife, Susan. We've been together since we were sixteen. Thirty eight years coming up soon.'

'That's great! That's exactly what'll happen to me and Graham.' She accepted the cigarette he offered. 'Thanks for coming along just then, by the way. I would have got totally drenched!' She pointed towards the road and they watched as the downpour increased.

Once again, Jack had to drop his speed. In the distance, the rumbling of thunder could be heard.

'They did forecast this you know.'

'I know, I know! Dad will be livid! Not exactly dressed for rain, am I?' She giggled as she looked down at her wet skirt.

'Nope. Still, I'm your knight in shining armour. Without me, you'd be walking up the aisle tomorrow coughing like anybody's business.' He signalled for

31

a green van to pull out in front of him. 'You might have to invite me to the wedding, you know,' he teased.

'But of course. Do come!' She looked at him seriously. 'Graham would love to meet you, I'm sure.'

'Is it a big wedding?'

'If everyone turns up we'll be 128 – that includes Nan. They're letting her out for the day.'

'I'm Jack, by the way.'

'Ellie. Pleased to meet you.' She giggled.

Ahead of them brake lights flashed and Jack's grip tightened around the steering wheel. For a while they were quiet as he concentrated on the driving.

'Just another few miles now and then you'll be home.'

'That's right. And only another fifteen hours and then I'll be Mrs Phillips. Can't wait!'

'Mrs Ellie Phillips, eh? It's got a nice ring to it.' Jack drew long and hard on his cigarette.

'Well it's better than Ellie Pond any day! I'm keeping my initials though.' She giggled again. 'You ought to come you know. My dress is absolutely gorgeous! Yards and yards of satin and the veil reaches right down to my ankles.' She moved her arms animatedly as she spoke. 'Mum's got me these lovely satin slippers too.'

'You'll be all right for the wedding waltz then. I should have had a pair of them. I was awful!' Jack groaned at the memory. 'I kept stepping on Susan's toes... and her mum's... and her aunt's... it was so embarrassing.'

32

Ellie laughed. 'Oh, we're not doing a proper waltz, you know. Although...' she pointed towards the radio, 'I might get Graham to dance to something smoochy, maybe by them...'

They listened in silence as 'A Hard Day's Night' came to an end.

'Yeah... Graham quite likes The Beatles... one of their slow ones will do. Nah! Who am I kiddin'? He hates dancing!'

The rain ceased. Jack switched off the wipers and opened the window a fraction.

Soon, cool night air filled the car. 'Any bridesmaids?'

'Five, as a matter of fact! There's Anna, Janet, Katy and Siobhan - they're my cousins - and Lottie, of course. She's my little sis'.'

'Next you're going to tell me it's top hats and tails!' Jack teased.

'Oh but it is! Mum wouldn't have it any other way. I can't wait to see Dad. He hates suits! He's convinced he'll look like a penguin!'

'Poor soul!'

'Oh... don't you worry about him! He does as he's told. Besides, it'll be great! Our family hasn't had a big wedding for yonks!' She sighed happily again, bringing her legs up and hugging her knees tightly.

Jack felt caught up in her excitement, not for the first time wishing that he and Susan had had kids.

'Afterwards, we've got the reception in 'The Lower Bell' you know,' Ellie continued. 'The whole place just for us. Imagine that!'

'You're a lucky lass, aren't you.' Their turn-off was just ahead of them and Jack slowed down to negotiate the bend by Blue Bell Hill. 'Here we are then, bride-to-be. Almost home…'

Turning to look at her, his smile froze as the car wheels screeched helplessly on the wet lane.

No! No! No-ooooooo!

Then a mighty bump. He heard himself scream, felt metal being crushed, saw a windscreen come towards him. And then… what was that? Staring eyes? Huge brown ones. Open really wide. And a gaping mouth? And the blood… oh the blood…

Was it real? Was it a dream? Was it his nightmare alive and kicking? Then nothing, just oblivion.

Jack's watch registered way past midnight when blue flashing lights lit up the darkness as two police cars arrived on the scene.

Jack felt totally drained. He knew he should get up, should walk towards the police cars. But he couldn't. He couldn't get up from the grassy bank. It was as if his brain wasn't quite up to issuing commands.

The mobile phone lay next to him. At least he had rung for help. Susan's line was still engaged.

His head hurt like hell. Concussion probably. And his right arm felt really weird.

Shrieks of laughter. Rain falling. I'm getting married in the morning…

'So…what's happened here then?' The voice belonged to a police officer coming towards him.

34

'I don't know, officer,' Jack confessed. 'It... I...'
He felt totally confused and very scared too. He was
supposed to remember something. Something
important. But what?

Car skidding. Too fast! Too fast!

'Can I see your licence, please?'

Jack fished it out of his wallet. The action made
him wince with pain. Perhaps his arm was broken?

'Would you mind?' Another officer pushed a
contraption under his nose.

'What? I'm not *drunk!* I've been to see a client!'
Jack felt indignant but obliged just the same,
satisfied to note that the breathalyser registered
negative. The third officer snorted and looked
disappointed.

'Going too fast, perhaps?' The officer scribbled
furiously in his notebook while the others, already
bored, returned to their cars.

No! No! Watch out! No-ooooooo!

'I was not! The roads are too slippery to go fast!'

Such ear-piercing screams. Crash! Bang!

'It's just, it's just... Christ!'

Huge brown eyes. Wide open; staring. Mouth
wide open; gaping. Blood trickling; red, then black.

Jack shook his head from side to side and looked
at the officer helplessly.

'It's just *what*?' The remark was sarcastic and
impatient.

Suddenly his brain kicked into gear again. 'Ellie.
That's it! It's Ellie. She... she's just... disappeared!'
He felt panic well up and look around him. 'She
must be here somewhere! You've got to find her!
She's probably hurt...'

35

'Are you saying someone was with you in the car?'

'Yes!'

The officer spoke quickly into his radio.

'One minute I was talking to her...' Jack continued. 'She's getting married tomorrow, you see - short dress, no long, satin veil, penguins, her Nan, all that jazz. Four, no five, bridesmaids I think she said.' He was babbling on and on. 'The reception's at the pub...' he pointed towards 'The Lower Bell' in the distance.

Someone sobbing. Someone moaning.

'And then the next minute, crash, bang.'

Then, eerie silence.

'I see. Hold on, please.' The officer moved back and went towards the police car nearest to him.

Jack could hear him speak quietly to the others.

'It's the truth... honest!' he shouted, feeling all panicky. 'Her name's Ellie Pond.' His head was throbbing. He looked at his car, still in the ditch, its bonnet crushed against the bank. There was no one in the passenger seat. 'I picked her up just outside Chatham,' he sobbed, fighting back nausea. 'She'd missed the last bus...'

The officer eventually returned.

'It's all arranged, Mr Parcell. We've called the garage; a recovery van will be here soon. Meanwhile we'll take you to Aylesford hospital for a quick check up. Everything's fine.'

'What do you mean *fine*?' Jack nearly choked on his words. 'You've got to find Ellie first. You hear!'

'I'm afraid we won't, Mr Parcell...' the officer sighed.

'What the hell do you mean?'

'Well… it looks very much like you gave a lift to Ellie Pond tonight.'

'I know I bloody did! I told you so myself!'

'So sad,' the officer continued, 'she was killed along this lane years back. 1965 I think it was… Night before her wedding and all. Must be her anniversary again...'

Déjà Vu
By Jillian Rawlings

It was a June scorcher. Dry heat seeped from the castle walls and what singed grass was left under the feet of the three o'clock tour surrendered to the dust. Guide books fanning their faces, a group of French students stood in a languid muddle and eyed the castle guide.

'I'm Alan,' he said, 'and I'm here to tell you about the castle.' He tried to make it interesting, even threw in a few French phrases and the odd joke, in English, which went right over most of their heads – smart little heads that, after seeing three picturesque ruins in the past week, had concluded that one pile of stones was much like another. Those that looked in his direction did so with vacant expressions of déjà vu – been here, seen it, done it all before. He knew just how they felt. This was his fourth tour today. Yes! He had been here, seen it and done it all before.

Conscious of bored feet scuffing the gravel, he made his move out of the Great Hall towards the northwest tower. 'Follow me,' he said with forced energy, 'I'd like to introduce you to some members of the castle household.' This was the part of the tour when he passed the group over to a couple of actors in costume for 'a theatrical experience'. Today it was Old Sir George and The Castle Cook, and good luck to them, he thought. Primary school groups and the more mature visitors were only too happy to play along, but knowing teenagers *en masse* did not do 'Let's pretend ...' It was not cool - certainly not on a sweltering day like today.

He glanced back at the group, ambling like lazy panthers and already nuzzling each other with the first purr of a giggle. The students swayed forward – all except one, a girl in a striped tee-shirt and dark trousers, who stood straight, eyes fixed on an upper window in the Great Hall. With a sudden jerk, her head twisted sideward towards the ruined battlements, as if someone, or something, had screamed for her attention. Her eyes darted, her lips trembled, her breathing became uneven and audible, so that others in the group turned towards her and she fell in a faint to the ground.

In the seconds before professionalism kicked in, Alan looked at the empty blackness of the small stone window, at the sunlight burning the parched weeds on top of the castle wall, searching for an explanation, but there was none.

'Move back. Give her a bit of space – and a little quiet, please.' The sleepy panthers were excited now, crowding round, chattering in animated French. The girl stirred and opened frightened eyes on Alan crouching beside her.

'Don't worry,' he said, 'It's just the heat – it's oppressive in here…' What a stupid thing to say, he thought, while half a dozen voices offered translation and bottles of mineral water. The girl sat up. She was trembling, shivering in shock.

'Sunstroke, most likely – coup de soleil,' Alan tried to appear casual. The girl's face was blanched beneath her sunburn and her arms were limp and cold. Someone came forward with a cotton shirt which Alan draped around her shoulders. She moved to get to her feet – to get away, Alan felt.

'Now, take it easy. Don't get up too quickly. There's no rush, but when you are ready, we'll move into the…' His hand gestured toward the tower behind the dark window.

The girl gasped and cowered back on the ground as if Alan were about to pick her up and throw her to the wolves.

'Non! Non! Le singe! Le singe est là! Non, non, non!

'MONKEY? What does she mean? Monkey? What monkey? Where?' chorused twenty french voices in various tones of interest, disbelief and amusement. Some of them began to make monkey noises – and lollop with swinging arms.

The girl saw that they were laughing at her, and Alan saw it too.

'That's enough! Now, please be sensible. You and…you,' he picked a young man and an older girl, the more serious-looking in the party, 'would you walk back to Reception with me and… er…

'Monique,' they volunteered.

'Yes – with me and Monique? Then the rest of you can continue your tour in the Undercroft. Cook is waiting for you.' He marched the party across the courtyard with surprising authority, and called, 'Cook! I have some helpers for you!'

Cook wasn't expecting anyone for at least five minutes, so appeared out of the vaulted gloom, surprised and flustered. 'Oh, dearie me!' she said, wiping her hands on her apron.' Well, well, come on in…'

Alan returned to Monique and the sensible pair, who were reassuring her and saying things such as, 'It must have been a shadow… a trick of the light…'But Alan knew by looking at Monique's face that it was no shadow nor a trick of the light. He knew exactly what it had been, even though he had seen nothing.

Just at that moment, aware that things were not running to schedule, Old Sir George appeared in full costume and bowed magnanimously, 'Friends and travellers…'

'We won't be needing the northwest tower piece today. Thank you Sir George.' Alan dismissed him in a tone that a lord of the manor might have used to a cold-calling double-glazing salesman. Old Sir George looked daggers under his wig and feathers and assessed the situation. Perhaps this was a particularly awkward party and Alan was saving him from them, but then .. poor Mary … coping as cook in the undercroft! How could Alan be so thoughtless!

'In that case, I shall go and discuss my supper with Cook,' and off he flounced to rescue Mary.

'How do you feel now, Monique? Alan asked.

'Much better.'

'Then shall we walk back to the office, where you can sit down and have something to drink?'

The sensible companions nodded and the four of them walked under the portcullis and over the drawbridge, back to the shop with its postcards and tourist gifts, and the children with ice creams playing on the grass.

The reception staff fussed over Monique, sat her with her feet up, offered a lavender stick to cool her brow and administered hot, sweet coffee.

'I'm not ill,' she said. 'You are very kind, but I am not ill. I have seen a ghost.'

Suddenly, the reception shop was heaving with activity. A group of elderly tourists arrived by one door, and the French students dribbled back through the other, loudly asking after Monique, and rifling through the postcards and tourist information.

'Please! Please! Is this one free? 'Is this one to pay for?' 'Please, how much this card?' 'Where to buy ice cream?' 'Please!' 'Please!'

The elderly group was hoping for a tour.

'Just a short tour – perhaps just the northwest tower? Alan, could you do it?' Sophie beseeched from behind the till.

Alan was glad to escape the chaos. 'No problem,' he said, 'Just follow me …'

This was the kind of tour he liked best – not so much a guided tour as a conversation with retired academics who knew their castles and their history. It would be an easy end to an exhausting day. Revelling in the atmosphere of the historic site, they chatted their way through nearly a thousand years, and found themselves standing outside the northwest tower.

'Would you like to meet Old Sir George?' said Alan, with the slightly raised eyebrow he used when inviting older visitors to play 'Let's Pretend ...'

'By Jove! I would! Wouldn't miss it for the world! Damn it, I probably know him!' said the joker amongst the academics, as they filed into the dark recesses of the northwest tower.

Old Sir George was a very able retired actor who spoke with thrilling tones and magnificent pauses. He could hold an audience spell-bound.

'Gather round,' he began, 'Enclose yourselves in the cool gloom of these ancient walls. Speak not a word but be still and silent in this eerie gloaming. Beware the black bending shadows. Beware the half-hidden hollows in the stone walls and the dark ways leading to blackness. Come closer now, and I will tell you a story that I have never told before, for the fear that in telling it I might unleash some awful force of evil.'

This was serious 'Man in Black' story-telling, and old Sir George already held his audience in the palm of his hand. He propped himself on a stool in front of them.

'I tell of a ruthless madman, Roland Rhys, who held court in the northwest tower of this castle with ... a Barbary ape – a wretched creature captured half-crazed from a shipwreck, and now enchained for entertainment.

On the night of which I speak a wind with the power of demons howled through the trees of Carew Park and rain lashed the castle with whips of wet steel. The ape grew restless in his chains, and Rhys grew morbid in the dull stupor of drink.

There was a knock at the great door. A Flemish tradesman, Horwitz, had made his way to the castle at the height of the storm, distressed and emotional, to tell how Rhys's son had forced entry to his home and raped his daughter.

In a drunken temper, Rhys loosed the ape's chains and goaded it to maul good Horwitz close to death.

Horwitz dragged himself free and slammed the door shut between himself and the maddened ape. Weak through loss of blood he struggled towards the castle gates and collapsed in semi-consciousness as piercing screams and groans rocked the castle walls. And then, smoke! Thick, acrid smoke!

Horwitz staggered to his feet. The northwest tower was ablaze. Dizzy with weakness, Horwitz made his way back into the smoking inferno, through the Great Hall where you have walked today, and there, in a pool of blood, he saw the figures of Rhys and the Barbary ape locked in mortal combat, a lighted taper in Rhys's hand torching all it touched.

Poor Horwitz summoned all his strength and fled, never to return, but the ghost of a tormented ape still haunts this castle, and the air in the northwest tower is tainted with the dank smoke of death.'

A moment of stunned silence was broken, after a respectful interval, by one of the academics.

'Bravo! An excellent story! Is it true?'

45

'Of course it's true!' said his wife, a fine-featured woman in a straw hat and long floral dress. 'Everyone knows that ghost stories are like pearls. False pearls become real as you wear them, and ghost stories become true as you tell them!'

'But...' Alan started to say something, but everyone was laughing, and this was Sir George's moment, so he walked back to Reception.

He was surprised to see the French party still there, just boarding their coach. Monique came up to him.

'You know, I did see a monkey.'

'Yes, I know you did.'

'You saw it, too?'

'No. No, I have never seen it,' he paused as Monique's dark eyes prompted him to continue, 'But...there is a story of a monkey – an ape – that was kept in the castle - for entertainment.'

'So, what I saw was his ghost.' Monique was not alarmed. She seemed reassured by Alan's directness.

'You know what, also,' she continued, looking deep into Alan's eyes, 'When I saw that that monkey, I smelt smoke.'

The students already on the coach were calling her.

'And you know what is more. I think as I walk round this castle that I have been here before. Déjà vu – as we say.'

'We say that too,' said Alan.

'Monique! Viens! Vite!' yelled her companions on the coach., but Monique stood still.

'And I am sure I will come back again.'

46

'I hope so,' said Alan. He took her hand and their fingers fused in uncanny empathy. He watched as she ran to the coach, and the driver revved away in a haze of diesel and dust.

It was shutting up time in the castle. Alan waited as the last of the academic visitors strolled through the gate and then fixed the chain and padlock.

'Busy day?' said the lady who had talked about the pearls. 'But you must feel so satisfied when you look back at the empty castle and think of all the pleasure you have given visitors.'

Alan smiled, but 'empty', he knew, was not the right word. Her husband joined her.

'Looks as if this hot spell is over. We're in for an almighty storm tonight!'

A low growl of thunder rolled round the hillside. They looked back at the castle as the shadows lengthened under gathering clouds.

'Empty!' thought Alan. 'Will this castle be empty tonight?'

And for the first time in one exceptional day he felt the icy fingers of fear grip his backbone.

Exposure
By David Peck

'Just go,' he'd said. Take the rest of the month to
think about yourself. Forget the department: we'll
manage without you. No email, no phone calls. I'll
see you on the first of December.

It hurt. For three years they'd worked together as
equals, the whole department strengthened by their
mutual respect. This felt like betrayal. But after a
weekend of soul-searching she understood his
concern; the need he'd felt to shock her into action.
Three months of frenetic twelve-hour working days
had been largely unproductive. Work had provided
an illusion of progress but her lack of direction since
the funeral had been obvious to everyone but herself.
She was inconsolable. Her mother's death was more
than she could bear.

Now, on a cold November morning in Snowdonia,
with sun shining on the Carneddeau and sparkling
on the still waters of Lyn Ogwen, she was ready to
take her first steps towards dealing with her loss.
Turning her back on the sunshine she crossed the
bridge behind Ogwen Cottage and took the path to
Cwn Idwal, the Devil's Kitchen and Glyder Fawr.
She would climb into sunshine on the ridge to Y

Garn and then leave the high contours to circle back to Ogwen: a walk she had first completed with her Welsh mother when she was eleven years old. She knew every step of the way.

Just thirty minutes of concentrating on putting one foot in front of the other on the rough slate path was enough to bring the memories flooding back. A detour above Lyn Idwal took her to the huge erratic boulder by the shore and her mother's voice describing the purple saxifrage which bloomed there in early spring. She remembered the story of the old blind farmer of Chapel Curig and his lifelong search for the Snowdon Lily. Hearing again the once familiar call of ravens in the Corrie, she raised her eyes to watch them tremble and swoop. Her mother's joy in their wild freedom had mirrored theirs. She wept.

Stumbling back to the main path she began the sharp climb through the Devil's Kitchen. Head pounding, breath coming in short gasps, she was again able to free her mind. Mum's death had come as a shock, mercifully, it had seemed at one time, she'd had little experience of bereavement. She searched her memory.

Twenty years ago she had encountered death on these very mountains. Walking with friends and growing tired of conversation she had left her companions behind temporarily, experiencing for herself the glory of a warm sunny morning.

Intrigued by a flash of colour from a nearby hollow she had gone to investigate. There, frozen as if in mid-stride lay the body of John Bryn Evans 51, a dental surgeon from Castle Walk, Chester. He was cold and dead, the wallet which identified him had fallen from his pocket, his glasses were broken, he lay in the short heather, his rucksack on his back. What mattered most was the expression on his face, still pink from the sun. John Evans was at peace, his last living moments spent as he might have wished; walking the mountains on a glorious morning.

She had sat with him for a while, feeling neither horror nor fear. In time she called her companions who took charge, calling police and mountain rescue. But she had continued her walk, wistful but not sad, strongly reassured by her experience.

A sharp gust of wind, causing her to stumble, brought her reverie to an end. A final sharp scramble brought her to the ridge. Time to rest, take a drink of tea, admire the still sunny crests of the Carneddeau and enjoy the peace. As if on cue, the snow began to fall. The blessed snow which captured silence and beautified all it touched.

She noted the heavy cloud over Snowdon and rose quickly to begin the ascent of Y Garn. The snow should not amount to much in November but she must make good use of the remaining hours of daylight. As she climbed she retreated again into memory, working patiently through the more significant moments of her life, re-living her relationship with her mother, recalling her strength, her independence, her love for others. But thought and memory gradually became less clear. Conscious now of cold seeping through her clothing she forced herself back to the present.

Confident in her knowledge of the route she had failed to check her position. The landmarks on which she had relied were now invisible through a cloud of swirling snow. In her rucksack were map and compass. She should stop and take her bearings but instinct told her to press on, beat the cold through rapid movement, get her circulation moving. She would walk fast for another thirty minutes and then take stock.

But weeks of overwork and interrupted sleep had left her weaker than she had realised. Tiredness gave way to exhaustion. The need to rest became irresistible. The cold snow promised relief, freedom from effort, peaceful sleep.

How long she slept she'd never know but she felt herself pulled into a sitting position. Hot tea and chocolate from her rucksack appeared in her hands. 'You've missed the path down to Ogwen', said a calm male voice. 'Stay on the ridge, don't deviate to the right. Wait for the first track to Bethesda, a long walk but the only safe way. Go now before the light fades.'

No time to waste she walked rapidly, thinking of the gathering darkness, aware of the sheer cliff to her right, taking care with each step. Once only she faltered, turning right drawn by the sound of heavy motors. The Bethesda Road? The calm male voice spoke again 'No it's the sound of the quarry 600 feet below. Retrace your steps to the path and continue north.' She did so without question, re-assured by his comforting presence.

In time the gradient beneath her feet changed. She had begun the slow descent to the track to Bethesda. She stopped, startled by the bark of a dog close by. A black and white border collie appeared through the gloom, barked again and then dropped to the ground in response to a sharp whistle from a man who then appeared, a radio receiver in his hand. 'I think we've been looking for you,' he said.

The story emerged as they talked in the Land-Rover on the way to Ogwen Cottage. David Griffiths, a Bethesda fireman had been exercising his dog on the lower slopes, secretly hoping the collie might be given an opportunity to use her hard won search and rescue skills when the message came, from Mountain Rescue. 'Strange call though' he said 'Guy called John Bryn Evans reported someone too close to the cliffs beyond Y Garn. Control said he seemed very relaxed but sure of himself. Never gave his own position, just went off.'

Outside the Snowdonia Café, Snowdon and the Glyders were outlined against the dying light to the West. Inside, steaming tea in pint pots, toasted teacake and a crowd of climbers reliving their day on the hill. Contemplation of death and near death experience could wait. She would make sense of it in good time. For the moment she was hungry. For life.

Druid's Hill
By Angela Williams

'Are you sure you want to go in? It's ten past five and I shut at six.'

The grey-haired lady in the ticket booth of the museum gave me a funny look. The postcards displayed on the rack next to the hatch window showed a creature with the torso of a man and a goat's head. This image contrasted sharply with the homely-looking museum attendant.

'It's all rubbish you know. I've worked here for eleven years and I don't believe a word of it. I've never even looked at the displays. It's just a load of old mumbo jumbo.' She adjusted her round specs and wrinkled her nose disapprovingly.

'Two tickets please.' I smiled, undaunted. As I handed over the money a sharp gust of wind picked up the five pound note and blew it out of my hand. I grabbed at the air but the money flew towards the back of the ticket booth.

'The magic's started already,' Liz giggled.

The lady selling the tickets did not smile. She counted out our change and added, 'I start cleaning up at quarter to six so I'll be up with my broom presently. You're bound to be my last customers.'

We crossed the threshold of the Museum of Witchcraft in Druid's Hill, Cornwall. In the distance I heard the roar of the sea as it crashed against the rocky cliffs. I was glad to be inside. Although it was mid-summer there was a powerful gale coming off the sea. The museum offered shelter from the ceaseless rain and hopefully some amusement. The interior of the museum was dimly lit and - judging by the way the wind whistled through the building - not well insulated. The first corridor we entered displayed etchings, drawings and paintings depicting anything to do with witchcraft.

'Molly, come and look at this.' Liz beckoned me towards a picture. The painting depicted the devil in his best known guise. He had long curling horns, a satyr's face and the hindquarters of a goat. He sat cross-legged on a throne, a great fire roared before him illuminating the night scene. His arms were raised heavenwards and he was surrounded by naked bodies in various stages of copulation.

'Well that's one way of keeping warm on a cold night,' I joked.

An etching next to the painting showed a young, dark-haired woman breast-feeding a black cat. The typed caption read: 'Witch suckles animal familiar. Familiars are traditionally witches' companions and can take on human form when it suits them. Witches were also accredited with the ability to take on animal form. A witch called Julia Cox, aged about seventy years, was indicted at Taunton, in Somerset,

56

in 1663, for transforming herself into a hare and for other sorcery.'

'So that's why my biology teacher used to smell of goats, she really was one in secret' Liz chuckled.

The next small drawing showed a nymph-like woman lying along the branch of an oak tree gazing up at the full moon. An owl glared out from between the branches. Underneath I read: 'Witches have often been associated with the pagan and nature religions. Worship of natural phenomenon such as trees and animals was believed to have been part of their ritual practice.'

We rounded the corner further towards the centre of the museum. A board with the word 'Spells' written in bold black letters hung above a glass cabinet. We gazed in wonder at the objects arranged in front of us. A selection of small cloth dolls sat in the glass cabinet, some with long steel pins stuck into them. Beside them I read: 'This spell was believed to get rid of a husband's lover. First, acquire a lock of hair or fingernail clippings of the offending woman. Make an effigy of her using these and then insert pins into offending areas.'

I giggled uneasily. I knew that Liz's long-standing boyfriend had recently had an affair. That was mainly the reason we had gone on holiday together, to try and cheer her up. Next to the cloth dolls stood a selection of long-necked, flat-bottomed, bulbous bottles.

'Look at this Liz, this is what the witches used to capture their farts in,' I read on, 'they thought the farts were evil spirits and wanted to save them to use at a later date. I wonder how on earth they did it.'

'I just feel sorry for whoever must have opened the bottles.'

'You never know, perhaps there are professional fart connoisseurs, like wine tasters, they can tell by one sniff in which year and by whom the fart was made.'

We rounded the next corner in the labyrinthian museum.

'Wait a minute,' Liz rummaged through her rucksack. 'Oh no, I think I must have left my purse at that tea house, I'll have to go back and look for it.'

'OK,' I replied, 'I'll wait here.'

My clothes felt cold and clammy. I rubbed my hands together in an effort to stimulate my circulation. In a glass cabinet opposite stood, entirely alone, a round swivel mirror. I walked over to take a closer look. Etched onto the surface of the mirror was a female face. I read the caption: 'There is an old witches' meditation technique which involves calling down the 'man in the Moon'. To exercise this technique one must position the mirror so that it reflects the full moon; gaze into it and the spirit of the moon will come down and inhabit the soul of the recipient. This mirror was the property of one Margaret Gilbert, a local healer who lived in the last century and was famed for her herbal remedies.'

I started to wonder about the person who had typed the captions in the museum. The ancient typewriter was faulty as every t and p jumped up a few millimetres above the other letters. It certainly couldn't have been the woman in the ticket booth; she had said she didn't believe in witchcraft. I suddenly had the sensation of being watched. I turned around and looked back down the corridor from where we had just emerged. Not a soul. Apart from the wind rattling through the building there was total silence. I turned around to look back at the mirror. In the distance I heard footsteps coming towards me. I felt relieved, thinking it was Liz returning. A young blonde-haired woman emerged from around the corner. She wore a long flowing skirt and cowboy boots. Her clothes and hair were dry so she couldn't have come from outside. I smiled and greeted her. She glanced at me, smiled and strode on, as if in a hurry. She disappeared into the adjoining corridor. She left behind a trail of perfume that I recognised. A scent I hadn't encountered for a long time; cheap perfume that reminded me of my schooldays. An advertising jingle sounded in my head and white handwritten letters spelling the name 'Charlie' flashed in front of me.

After what seemed like forever, Liz returned, soaked again and breathless. 'My purse was still on the table. Thank God nobody had taken it. It would have been a real hassle if my credit cards had gone missing.'

'Did you pass anyone as you left the museum?' I asked.

'No, only that funny old biddy at the entrance, she was chatting to an old man, a local wizard I expect. Why?'

'Oh, no reason, just thought I'd heard some other people walking around that's all.'

We wandered on to the next display; two mannequins in bikinis wearing cat masks next to a mock tree decorated with lots of little plastic babies. I cleared my throat nervously, 'This is really weird.'

'This museum reminds me of some tacky Saturday night horror movie' Liz responded.

'Shall we move on, it's getting late and we'd better see about finding a bed and breakfast for tonight?' I suggested.

We walked back towards the entrance. Ahead of us I heard the swish, swish of the ticket-seller's broom against the floorboards as she cleaned up for the day. I imagined her diligently sweeping the dust away, her head firmly down, refusing to look at any of the displays. We startled her as we came around the corner. Concealing her moment of alarm she straightened her pinny. Resting on her broom, she peered at us over her glasses. 'You're all finished are you? I'll see you out then. I've locked up downstairs already.' She led us back through the museum and out of the front entrance.

'Do you know of any B&B's around here?' I asked.

'Well you could try Mrs Thompson, she lives in the white house at the top of the hill; follow that road up there.' She pointed to a road that led up the side of the cliff.

We set off in that direction. She stood in the doorway and watched us walk away. When we were about a hundred yards away from the museum I looked back. She hadn't moved and was still stood at the doorway, broomstick in hand. I raised my hand to wave and as I did so a black cat shot out from behind the wall surrounding the museum, raced towards the door, brushed past the old lady's legs and disappeared into the darkness of the building. She smiled, turned and closed the door.

The brass knocker was in the form of a Cornish pixie. I knocked twice. An aging but well-dressed woman opened the door. I asked if any double rooms were available.

'You're in luck; I've got a double room with twin beds, just for two nights mind you. It's booked up for the weekend.'

I couldn't quite place her accent. 'Great, could we see the room?' I responded.

'It's got a lovely view of the sea. Follow me and I'll show you,' Mrs Thompson laid down the bundle of fresh herbs she had just picked, on the hallway table. Her slim, upright form led us up the carpeted stairs. She opened the door and walked towards the french windows that looked out onto the grey, turbulent sea.

'Lovely, isn't it? This is one of the best views in the whole of Cornwall, and only fourteen pounds a night.' She made a theatrical gesture towards the window.

I walked over to one of the beds and tested its springiness. Mrs Thompson gave me a disapproving look. 'Those beds are new; I bought them just after New Year. Unlike a lot of people in these parts offering bed and breakfast, I believe in investing in my business.'

'Quite.' I stood up feeling admonished. 'As far as I'm concerned it's fine, what about you Liz?'

'Yes, it looks really comfortable.' Liz would rather die than ever complain about anything.

'A full Cornish breakfast tomorrow?', asked Mrs Thompson as she replaced a lock of hennaed hair that had escaped from her bird's nest bun.

'Yes please,' we nodded in unison.

'I'll leave you to settle in then. Breakfast is from seven till nine. There is a television lounge for the guests downstairs. If you want tea and coffee, just ask.'

We both slept well and awoke the next morning to the smell of bacon and coffee wafting up the staircase. After we'd eaten Mrs Thompson refilled our coffee cups. 'What are your plans today ladies?' She enquired.

'Well, we'd thought about going into Tintagel. Are there any buses going in that direction?' I asked.

'My son will run you in, he works in Tintagel. He leaves in about half an hour. That should give you enough time to get ready.'

Outside we clambered into an old coffee-coloured Ford Capri. The air-freshener failed to mask the smell of petrol and grease.

'She may be old, this one, but she still goes. All she needs is a bit of loving attention.' He patted the dashboard affectionately. Mrs Thompson's son Les, turned round and winked at us. His glance lingered for longer than was strictly necessary on Liz. She often had that effect on men. I knew that she only had eyes for one man, but he had let her down. Les started the car. He drove very fast along a narrow, winding road flanked by overgrown hedges. He told us that he worked as a mechanic in a garage in Tintagel.

'I love machines,' he added, 'I understand machines.' He turned the radio up so loud it made conversation quite hard and after passing some inane pleasantries we were all silent. In Tintagel Les drove into King Arthur's car park.

'I'll be leaving about half past four. Do you want a lift back?'

'Well, we'll see. If we're not here don't wait for us. We're used to finding our own way around. Thanks anyway.' He waved as he disappeared into a narrow alley away from the car park.

'He's a bit old to still be living with his mother isn't he?' remarked Liz. 'He must be forty-five if he's a day. Funny really because his mother looks very young for her age.'

'Come on,' I felt a sudden urge to run as the breeze off the sea rushed over my cheeks, 'let's go and explore.'

We climbed up the wooden steps that led to Tintagel Castle perched high up on a rocky promontory. This was King Arthur's alleged birthplace. We reached the top and walked onto an outcrop of rock that was covered in moss and lichen. The castle itself was little more than a few broken down walls but the view over the sea was breathtaking. Just for a few brief seconds the clouds parted and the sun broke through. The sea changed colour and momentarily reflected the bright blue of the sky in its calm, mirror-like surface. I looked back towards the jagged face of the cliff. A movement on the cliff top caught my eye. A woman was walking along its edge. Her wide skirt billowed behind her.

Her long blonde hair streamed in the wind like some victorious golden flag.

'It's her again, the Charlie woman.' I turned round to discover that Liz was no longer standing next to me. She'd climbed up onto the castle wall and was gazing out at the water. When I glanced back at the cliff the woman had gone.

After the castle we explored the town and when our feet started to ache we stumbled into Guinevere's teashop. Liz was starting to relax. She didn't give any sign that she was thinking about her ex's betrayal. I too felt relaxed and content, only somewhere in the back of my mind was the memory of the young woman I'd seen striding through the museum and on the clifftop today. It bothered me.

'Do you believe in ghosts?', I asked casually as I sipped my tea.

'Don't know really, don't think so. Do you?'

'Depends a bit. There's something magical here in Cornwall. I know it's tacky and commercial the way they cash in on the King Arthur legend, but beneath all that there is something here, something mystical. It's like a lot of Celtic countries, they say the air is thin; there are all sorts of doorways into the other world.

Liz raised her eyebrows 'Mol, you've been visiting too many witches' museums.'

I poked my tongue out at her. Sometimes Liz's down-to-earth reactions were the perfect antidote for my imagination. Although it had led to friction between us in the past, I was glad of her scepticism at that moment. I didn't want to believe in anything supernatural. The woman I'd seen at the museum and on the clifftop was just someone on holiday like us. This aura of strangeness around her existed purely in my imagination

'I think I'll go up to bed, I'm whacked.'

'OK, I'll be up shortly. Goodnight.' Liz left me alone in the television lounge and went up to bed. I heard someone run down the stairs and go out through the front door. The light outside started to fade. It was June 21st, the longest day, Summer Solstice. I'd nearly finished my book and was determined to complete it before going to bed. I don't know how long I stayed up reading but as I turned the last page, without warning, the lights went out. I waited a while until my eyes acclimatised to the gloom. A faint light shone briefly from outside the window. A shadow walked past. I waited a while, half expecting Mrs Thompson to appear with candles, but she failed to materialise. Well, I'll just have to feel my way up to my room. Perhaps Liz had packed a torch, I thought hopefully.

I opened the door and walked out to the carpeted hallway. The grandfather clock in the hall chimed once. It was much later than I had realized. I groped my way to the wooden banister and felt its cold, smooth surface under my hand. I stepped carefully, feeling the way with my feet. At the top of the stairs a pale oblong of light flooded onto the floor. Outside, above a row of fir trees a full moon shone brightly. I thought of the round mirror in the witches' museum and the calling down the moon ceremony. As I gazed out a sudden curtain of dark indigo clouds passed over the moon's face and once again the landing was flooded in darkness. Next to my feet, beneath the wooden skirting board I heard a furtive scratching. I knew it was only mice but it unnerved me. Which was our room, was it the first or the second door on the left? There was a scratch board picture of an owl hanging on it, but that wouldn't be much help to me in this darkness. I edged my way along the landing, feeling my way along the wall, then I felt a round doorknob under my fingers. Yes, it was the first on the left, I'm sure of it; I turned the knob, creaking the door open.

'Liz, are you there?' I whispered.' Liz it's me, wake up. There's been an electricity cut. Do you remember packing a torch?' As I completed my sentence the landing light came back on again. It cast enough light to illuminate the room I was peering into and I realised it was the wrong one. I know I should have shut the door but I flicked on the light switch instead. I saw an unmade single bed, a poster of a football team on the wall and clothes strewn all around. It looked like a teenager's room; the sort of room that mother was banned from. On the table next to the bed was a cup. A green layer of mould had settled on the top of the coffee coloured liquid. There was a sour smell of unwashed clothes. The contrast with the rest of the house was startling. I felt some silly urge to start tidying up. I'd worked part-time as a cleaner when I was a student and I suppose old habits die hard. There were a few hardback books on the window ledge and stacked between them a photo album. I guiltily remembered the times I used to peep into people's albums when I tidied their houses. It was the only thing that made the work interesting.

66

I walked over to the window and picked up the album. I turned over the stiff pages. There were the usual photos of weddings, Christmas parties. It all seemed terribly normal. There were photos of Les as a young boy, with his football team. Next to that was Mrs Thompson standing next to a winning cake at a W.I competition. It was obviously an old photo. She wore a fifties style two-piece suit. She looked different somehow, less bitter. I turned the pages, not really knowing what I was looking for. And then, near the end of the album I found it. Les with his arm around the blonde-haired woman I'd seen in the museum. They looked adoringly into each others eyes.

I stood there looking at the photo for some time. A moth had started pattering around the light bulb. I was just going to shut the album when I spotted the yellowed edge of a newspaper cutting peeking out from the pleated wallet inside the back cover. I pulled it out and read the headline: "RECENTLY ENGAGED YOUNG WOMAN KILLED IN CAR CRASH." The article continued: "Isobel Grayson, a locally known white-witch who dabbled in healing and herbal remedies, was fatally injured in a car crash last Friday. The brakes of her car were believed to have been faulty. The police suspected that Miss Grayson was the victim of foul play as she had allegedly been mixed up with a witches' coven. She had recently received a voodoo doll in her image." I read the date at the top of the page, 30th June, 1970. The Charlie girl smiled out at me from the photo.

Downstairs I heard the front door slam shut. My fingers trembling I put the cutting back in the album. I turned off the light and shut the door. I heard voices downstairs, Les and Mrs Thompson. I hid behind the wardrobe on the landing as I heard footsteps coming up the stairs. Outside Les's room mother and son embraced each other. The beat of my heart was so powerful I half expected it to explode out of my chest. I felt the sweat break out on my palms and then thankfully mother and son released one another and went to their rooms. I stumbled to my room and was a little comforted by the sound of Liz's regular breathing. I closed the curtains, got undressed and dived into bed.

I drifted in and out of sleep. As dawn was starting to glimmer through the curtained window I was awakened by the sound of female laughter. I shivered under the duvet. I was glad we were leaving in the morning. Suddenly I couldn't wait to get away.

At breakfast I just ate some cereal and toast. Liz had a full cooked breakfast but the smell of it turned my stomach. Mrs Thompson looked tired as she served our food. She looked her age. Her hair hung loose and the grey roots showed. Her eyes were puffed and she had dark circles under them as if she hadn't slept. Les popped his head around the door.

'Want another lift into town ladies? I'm leaving in about ten minutes.' His gaze was aimed at Liz and once again his eyes lingered upon her. I half expected his tongue to drop out of his mouth. His mother was pouring out a coffee but she too noticed the look that her son directed at Liz. Anger and jealousy passed over her face like dark clouds. The blood drained away from her lips. Coffee spilled onto the white linen as the cup ran over.

'Mrs Thompson, look out, you're spilling the coffee.' exclaimed Liz.

'Oh yes, sorry, how clumsy of me.' She reached for a table napkin and mopped up the stain. She regained her composure and forced a smile onto her lips. It looked more like a grimace. 'Les my dear, the ladies are leaving today, I'm sure they've got other plans, I expect they've seen enough of Tintagel.'

'Yes, we're heading for Land's End today,' replied Liz, 'but thanks for the offer.' She smiled at Les, oblivious of the effect she was having.

'You'd better go now Les,' commanded Mrs. Thompson, 'you know I asked you to do some shopping for me today before you start work, now be off with you.'

'Bye,' he muttered and left, like a scolded child.

'That's my boy,' Mrs. Thompson said to herself, as she stacked the plates and cleared up the breakfast table. 'That's my boy.'

The Blue Lady
By Sandy Neville

Two uniformed men and a lady are standing by our front door. There's a military police car parked nearby. I grab hold of Mum's hand, my stomach churning. I know why they're here.

*   *   *

Earlier that Sunday, the first weekend of the school holidays, there had been no hint of what was to happen. We stopped to eat our picnic, sitting on the bank of a gurgling stream.

'Yuk, this cheese tastes horrible.'

Despite his moaning, Jamie carried on chewing his sandwich. He's my brother and he's nine. He bosses me about, 'specially when Dad's away.

My name's Mark. I'm seven. I like football, swimming and most sports. I hate reading, vegetables and my brother.

Mum, she's a bit podgy with curly hair and a nice face, leant against the trunk of a willow tree, eating an apple. She'd decided on the walk because she's on another diet and trying to exercise. Dad, who's fighting the Argies in the Falklands, will be

71

home soon – whoopee!. Mum wants to be thin so he'll still love her.

I ran over to read a signpost next to a stile, 'Footpath to Abbey and Hall'.

'Wow, so you can read all by yourself,' Jamie said. 'It sounds a mega boring place.'

But it certainly wasn't boring. At first it was brilliant. We walked over stepping stones. The water wasn't deep and was so clear that I could see loads of little silvery fish. Mum rolled up her trousers and took off her sandals. 'In case I fall in,' she said. She laughed as she jumped from stone to stone. She hardly ever laughs when Dad's away. Me and Jamie splashed each other. Mum didn't even mind that we got wet.

We bought ice cream at the café and chucked bits of cornet into the water for the ducks.

We set off again, me and Jamie running in front. The Abbey in the distance was all white pillars and arches against the blue sky. The monks used to live there but now a lot of the building has collapsed.

'Just a minute,' Mum shouted. I turned. She was standing by some trees.

When we ran back, Mum pointed to a big, old building, close by, surrounded by trees

'That's the Hall,' she said. 'Let's go and look round.'

The Hall was high, built of grey-white stone. Towers were at the corners, like castle battlements. The narrow windows set into the stone walls made me shiver. It was as if eyes were watching from behind the glass.

In front of a heavy wooden door sat a fat, smiley lady.

'You've got the place to yourselves. Most folk are out in the sun,' she said as she handed Mum a guide book. Then she ruffled my hair with sausage fingers, like I was a kid. I hate that.

The door led into a cold, dark hall. Suits of armour stood to attention in the corners. There were heads of dead animals, deer, a fox and a wild boar, staring sadly into the distance from the rough stone walls.

I shivered. It felt creepy. Mum looked at the guide book. 'We won't be here long,' she said. 'There are only two rooms open to the public.' She led us to the morning room. It was very big, with high decorated ceilings. There were paintings of miserable people dressed in dark clothes. Their eyes told us to get out of their house.

Mum wandered about looking at the pictures and her guide book. All the time I wanted to run outside to the sunshine.

At last Mum led us back into the dreary hall and towards room number two – the library.

As soon as we got to the doorway, my legs didn't want to walk any further. I knew that I shouldn't go into that room. It was icy cold – and voices were murmuring in the background. I couldn't hear what they were saying.

Jamie shoved me and suddenly I was inside the library. It was much darker than the previous room, mainly because of all the wood shelves and dull covered books. It smelt musty. The voices were louder but still I couldn't make out any words.

'Where are those voices coming from?' I asked. Mum and Jamie looked at me as if I'd gone daft.

'Voices? You're hearing things.' Mum pointed to a big painting over the mantelpiece.

'That picture over there...' Her voice faded into the distance.

All I could hear was the ticking of a grandfather clock. I jumped as it chimed twice.

Even though I didn't want to go, my legs took me to a particularly cold, dark corner of the room. To my surprise, standing next to one of the bookcases was a lady dressed in a long, blue, shiny dress. She turned and looked at me. Her brown hair was tucked into a blue bonnet. Her face was beautiful but oh, so sad. A tear rolled down her cheek.

She seemed to be trying to talk to me. Her lips moved but I couldn't hear what she was saying.

'You'll have to speak up,' I said. I walked closer. Still I heard nothing. The lady shimmered, like a tarmac road on a hot day, and disappeared. In her place I could see Dad. He was there, there in the library. He smiled. 'Tell Mum I will be home,' he said. I tried to smile back... something was wrong. Then I saw the blood, so much blood, and screamed.

'It's very kind of you to give us a lift,' Mum said to the fat lady.

'No problem, Love,' the lady said. 'I only hope the little lad is okay.'

Mum stroked my face. 'Been out in the sun too long, I reckon,' she said.

'Just round this next bend and we'll be home'.

The lady nodded. 'Funny, another kiddie got all upset in that room a while ago. It's s'posed to be haunted you know. A blue lady – load of nonsense if you ask me.'

Mum laughed. 'Well there wasn't any blue lady today. James and I were there the whole time and saw nothing. Isn't that right, Jamie?'

My brother nodded.

Our house came into view.

'There are some people standing by the front door,' Jamie said.

The phone rings and one of the policemen answers. He listens for a long time.

'Thanks,' he says and puts the phone down.

He looks at Mum. 'That was the latest on your husband. He's extremely poorly.' Then he looks at me and Jamie. 'Do you want the children to stay?'

I hold Mum's arm very tightly, so does Jamie, 'Please Mum,' I say, and she nods.

The policeman tells us that Dad has been hurt in an explosion. He's just had an emergency operation to stop him bleeding. His heart did stop, about an hour ago, during the operation. I look at the time – it's just after three o'clock. It was two o'clock, an hour ago, when I saw Dad in that cold library. The man says the doctors managed to revive him. He is still very ill though.

Mum and Jamie start to cry. I don't, 'cause I know that Dad is going to get better. I'll tell Mum and Jamie about it later, about Dad and about the blue lady that only I could see. I hope they'll believe me and stop being sad

The Devil In My Bed
By Sasha Fenton

It is not often that something that I read keeps me
awake. My only previous experience of sleep
deprivation had been brought on by an imaginative
idea that had occurred almost forty years earlier. My
then husband, Tony Fenton, was a good sleeper. He
was also an avid reader, but nothing that he read
ever played on his mind. One night he was
obviously disturbed, because he spent it muttering,
shouting and throwing the bedclothes around. The
next morning, I asked him what had disturbed him
so badly. He said that he had been upset by a book
that he had just finished reading. He handed me the
book and I read it. After this, I spent the next three
nights walking around, lighting cigarettes and
drinking tea to calm myself. It is doubtful that the
same book would upset anyone to the same extent
now, but then it presented a frightening and all too
likely prospect. What was the book? It was called
'On The Beach' and it was by the great Australian
writer, Neville Shute.

The story concerned two people who discovered that
they were in love at a truly awkward moment in
time. The Cold War had hotted up to the point where

the United States, Soviet Union and much of Europe had bombed itself into oblivion. Neville Shute was obviously aware of something, which up to that point had escaped the attention of ordinary people. He speculated that following a nuclear holocaust, atomic radiation would be caught up in the clouds and then spread around the world, gradually poisoning one country after another. At the start of the story people in northern Australian cities were being treated for radiation damage. Some were moving southwards in search of a few more precious weeks of life, while others had already accepted the inevitable. One wry comment that remains in my mind to this day was that the hated Australian rabbits were likely to survive a year longer than the population.

The hero and heroine lived on a peninsula that lies to the south east of Melbourne. This is about as far south as one can go without leaving the Australian mainland. The southerly latitude and distance from the northern hemisphere only offered them time to contemplate their fate, but no escape from it. Eventually the invisible miasma reached them, and the story closed with the couple sitting on Dromana Beach, appreciating the beauty of the place, while they spent their last few hours of health and happiness in each other's arms.

A few short years after Tony and I had read this story, the photographs taken from Apollo Eleven showed us just how fragile our earth and its atmosphere truly are. Suddenly everyone could see that atomic radiation would not roll slowly down the earth from north to south, but that it would swirl around against the rotation of the earth until it covered every place within a matter of days. When we saw those first beautiful pictures of our world, Tony and I felt even worse about the dreadful prospect that Neville Shute had postulated.

Many years later, when the nuclear threat had long gone, fate took us to Sydney and then on to Melbourne. While in Melbourne, we became friendly with a local radio presenter called Michael. Michael invited us to spend one of our free days taking a trip by train to his home town of Port Arthur. He met us at the station and took us for lunch, and then drove us around on a tour of the area. As a pleasant break from all the riding around he took us to a lovely beach. We were strolling along and admiring the hilly landscape behind the beach and the light on the sea, when Michael casually mentioned that the place was called Dromana Beach. He could not understand why Tony and I suddenly stopped stock-still and stared at one another white-faced. When we explained what had upset us it did not really get through to Michael. He did not belong to the generation who had lived through the terrifying threat of nuclear war, so this place did not represent the end of the world to him in the way that it did to us.

*   *   *

The second time that something that I read kept me awake was just before Christmas 2003. One night, shortly before falling asleep, I had been reading a silly article in a magazine. In this article, three women insisted that they had been visited by the Devil. Apparently, the Devil had climbed on top of them during the night and made love to them. I would normally have forgotten this article soon after reading it but I had not bargained for what happened to me that night.

My present husband, Jan Budkowski, is a poor sleeper and he often works late into the night, so I had gone to bed at my usual time while Jan continued to work. Before falling asleep I had felt slightly disturbed by a 'presence' that I sensed hovering in the corner of the room. I am a medium, so ghostly visitations do not frighten me, but up until then I had never had a ghostly lodger in my bedroom. I was very tired, so I ignored the vague aura in the room and promptly fell asleep.

A couple of hours later I was suddenly shaken awake by a dull thud and the knowledge that a substantial body had landed heavily on Jan's side of the bed. My side of the bed actually moved up slightly while the counter-weight of the heavy body pushed the mattress down on the other side. I knew this was not Jan because he is not heavy enough to displace the mattress – and anyway, he always slides gently into bed so as not to wake me. This was something else. In my dopey state, the stupid Devil story shot into my mind and frightened me.

I sat up quickly and turned on the light. It took a moment for me to register that there was nobody in my bed or in the room, and it took a few moments longer for my heart to stop pounding. I wrote the experience off to the silly magazine article and to eating cheese for supper. My mother used to say that eating cheese late at night leads to bad dreams, so that was clearly the answer. That would have been the end of the story but the 'presence' still hung around the house, and it continued to haunt me on and off throughout Christmas – although not as dramatically as on that night. On three separate occasions I heard footsteps walking into my office and the slight squeak that my office chair gives when someone sits down heavily on it. When I looked in my office, of course there was nobody there.

Immediately after Christmas, I had an out-of-the-blue phone call from a woman whom I had last seen many years before. Indeed, the caller had still been a schoolgirl when I had last seen her. This was Valerie, and she was the eldest child of a man called Malcolm who had been my first boyfriend during my teenage years. The romance was over by the time I was nineteen, but Malcolm and I had remained good friends ever since and we had always helped each other out in times of trouble.

Malcolm had always felt more for me than I had for him. Although he had not said much at the time, I was aware, both before I married Tony and at times when my marriage was difficult, that Malcolm was standing in the wings. I always knew that he would have gladly married me. I knew I could never feel enough for Malcolm to make him happy, but I loved him enough not to want to make him unhappy. I knew that if I had married him out of loneliness I would have destroyed our friendship for no purpose.

Malcolm and I were always there for each other in times of need, and we both truly appreciated the deep friendship that endured over so many years.

I had intended to give Malcolm a call before Christmas for a good old gossip, but what with one thing and another I didn't get around to it. Valerie told me that two days before Christmas, Malcolm had had a massive stroke during the night and that he had died in his sleep. After I put the phone down and gave myself a little time to absorb this sad fact, I realised who it was that had visited my bed and that was walking into my office.

Malcolm was not the sort of person who talked about his ailments and he had only ever opened up to Valerie, so I had not known how sick he was. Although in his early sixties, he was still at work and he had an active social life. He was an old soldier who had never really left the army. He still trained young men to play music in the Guards Band, and he kept busy as the secretary of the Grenadier Guards' Association. Malcolm knew he had problems, but he had clearly not expected his life to end so suddenly.

As a medium, I know that those who die unexpectedly are often disorientated and that they will throw out cries for help to those who knew them when they were alive. Malcolm had perhaps tried to contact his children and maybe other relatives as well, but they would not have picked up the message. A medium has an antenna for this sort of thing, so it was not surprising that I had picked up the call, especially as the fondness between us still existed. Some gentle questioning confirmed that

Malcolm's arrival in my bed must have taken place a few moments after he had died.

Owing to the holiday season, Malcolm was still waiting to be buried. We all know that burial is no guarantee that a person will 'go over' and stop haunting the living - but for most people it is the cut-off point from this life and the time when they feel free to start their journey into the next life.

Valerie phoned to tell me the date of the funeral, and then she told me a strange story. Valerie and her two younger brothers had had no choice but to clear Malcolm's flat immediately after Christmas. It had been 'tied' to his job and now the owners would need to find a replacement for Malcolm and they would need the flat for the new man. Malcolm came across to others as a cool and logical person, but he had clearly had many deep feelings that he had kept to himself. Valerie and her brothers were amazed to discover that he had kept photographs, including those of their mother, Malcolm's first wife, along with many other unexpected mementos, including some from me.

After some hours of work they decided to take a break for lunch, so they locked up and went out. There was only one lock on the door and only one key. There was also a rusty old bolt that had not been used for years as it could not be moved. When the three returned to finish clearing the flat, they discovered that their key turned but that the door would not open. They called for help and eventually someone came and broke into the empty flat. The bolt had been pushed home from the inside!

I explained to Valerie that Malcolm had always valued his privacy and that he had felt his home and property to be sacrosanct. He had tried living with their mother, a subsequent wife, and probably one or two other women, but that he had only been truly happy on his own. In his disturbed and confused state he must have become angry at seeing his things being turned over and removed.

Realising that Malcolm must be very upset, later that day I 'tuned in' and connected with him. I told him what had happened and I explained that he would soon have to leave his old life behind and to look for the light and follow it to Heaven. I suggested that he might like to stay around for his funeral, because I knew that Valerie and his sons were arranging something special for him, even to the point of playing some amusing passages from the Goon Shows that he had loved.

The following evening the television ran a documentary about the Second World War. Malcolm and I had always shared an interest in history, particularly military history, and we had often talked about these things with each other. That evening Jan was busy so I sat down to watch the programme by myself. I was not surprised when I felt a presence close to me. I mentally told Malcolm that he was welcome to sit with me and watch the programme and then to stay near me until his transition if that made him feel better. I felt his presence around the house off and on for the next few days, especially in my office, which is my own personal space in the house. Then the funeral date passed and my house 'cleared'.

Now my house is clear of old boyfriends and there have been no more bodies landing in my bed. If any more bodies turn up next to me at least I will know that it is not the Devil dropping in for a night of passion!

Last Year's Doll
By Liza Granville

It had looked simple enough on the map, but the instant Jane turned into the cul-de-sac she knew the short cut had been a mistake.

She stopped. One quick glance took in the jagged car wrecks, the mountain of split bin-bags, the wary slink and dart of an army of half-starved cats. The place stank of decay and neglect: a last outpost of misery on the fringe of a chic new housing estate.

Every instinct warned her to turn back. Instead, she braced herself. After all, the map was right: the entrance to the narrow alley was only yards away. Beyond it towered the sleek outlines of the office complex. This route would save her at least ten minutes. Besides, if she turned back now she'd probably be late. When you'd just landed your first real job, that wasn't a risk worth taking.

The house whose spiky hedge formed the left side of the alley was even grimmer than the rest, crouching in a pool of shadow so intense that the building seemed to be generating its own cankerous darkness. The walls were stippled every shade of grey, from clinker at the bottom to dirty silver under the eaves. Ugly black lichens mottled the roof. Ash-coloured net curtains strained across the windows. Even the tired grass was tinged with charcoal.

A miasma of hopelessness hung over the place.

Jane shrank. Her spirits plummeted. She shivered, suddenly realising how eerily quiet it was here, as if that shadow was also reaching out to absorb every sound. Only the quickening tap of her heels broke the blanketing silence. And it was so cold, too. In spite of the bright spring sunshine, a bitter mid-winter chill borne, perhaps, on a stray wind, was gnawing through to her bones.

As she reached the corner, a tiny stick insect of a child materialised, clinging for dear life to the slowly swinging gate. She was incredibly dirty: gummy-eyed, her hair an uncombed bird's nest tangle, and dressed in a ragbag assortment of ill-fitting hand-me-downs. Jane averted her eyes. Somebody ought to do something. You heard such stories…

'Hello.'

It would have been so easy to ignore such a faint whisper. The sound was hardly louder than an out-breath. Jane glanced back with a brief, tight smile. Then she saw the pleading in the child's eyes and relented, injecting as much warmth as she could into her answering, 'Hello there!'

She was rewarded with a smile of pure joy before the little girl shyly disappeared.

Emerging into the sunshine again, Jane glanced at her watch. Better than she'd expected: coming that way had saved almost fifteen minutes. And it hadn't been that bad. Not really.

There was no sign of the child on the way home, but the next morning she was there again, still unwashed, still balanced on the gate, still wearing the same grubby pink tee-shirt over stained leggings. As Jane had stepped off the bus the road had already been shimmering with the intense heat. Here it was positively arctic. She couldn't stop shivering.

'Hello again. What's your name?' A bit feeble, she thought. But Jane didn't have much to do with small children and couldn't think of anything else to say.

'Kylie.' This time the whisper was accompanied by an endearingly shy, gap-toothed smile. A grubby hand came from behind her back, clutching a few wilted forget-me-nots. 'I picked them for you.'

The tiny fingers felt like icicles. Jane reluctantly poked the flowers into her top buttonhole.

'They're lovely,' she lied, 'What a nice surprise. And it's not even my birthday. When's your birthday, Kylie?'

'Tomorrow.'

'Tomorrow? That's exciting. D'you know what you're getting?'

The child stared at her so blankly that for a moment Jane wondered if she was quite all there. Then, with a sick lurch, she realised that the little girl didn't expect to be given anything.

'Well,' Jane gabbled, angry with herself, wishing the words unsaid, 'If you could have anything in the world, anything at all, what would you wish for?'

'A doll,' breathed Kylie, her eyes shining, 'A doll with yellow hair like yours.'

89

The gift shop in the arcade had a huge selection of dolls. None of them was exactly what Jane was looking for. They were all too modern, too adult. At last she found the right one, a traditional baby girl with china-blue eyes and blonde ringlets, tucked away at the back of a shelf.

'You're in luck,' beamed the assistant, 'That one's been reduced. It's nearly half price.'

Jane hesitated. From the look of things, Kylie already had enough second-bests. If she was going to do this, it might as well be done properly.

'Why? What's wrong with it?'

'Nothing at all. It's just old stock. One of last year's dolls.'

Perhaps that wouldn't matter.

'Happy birthday, Kylie.' Jane clutched her jacket round her and tried to stop her teeth chattering. 'Look, I've got a little present for you, but I really ought to see your Mummy first.' The last thing she wanted was for her gift to be misconstrued.

'Our Mum's not here. She's gone.'

'Shopping?'

Kylie shook her head. She tore away the wrapping paper and stared at the doll with shining eyes. 'For me?', she checked anxiously, holding it against her thin chest, 'For ever?'

'For ever and ever!' Jane smiled, enjoying her fairy godmother role, even whilst she shivered, and stamped her feet to keep them warm. 'I have to go to work now, Kylie. Tell your Mummy I'll pop in and see her on my way home.'

The little girl nodded and scuttled off to be absorbed by the dense shadow at the side of the house.

'See you soon,' murmured Jane. But that evening she worked late and couldn't bring herself to brave the shortcut at twilight. The next morning she overslept and her mother insisted on driving her to the office, so it wasn't until the following afternoon that she made the promised attempt to speak to Kylie's mother.

The instant Jane reached the passageway she saw that something terrible had happened. Kylie's house was a wreck. The walls were blackened. The front door was blistered and charred. Every window was boarded over. Heaps of furniture mouldered on the front lawn.

Kylie? A hand seemed to clutch at Jane's heart. It was only when she felt the cold dread settle in the pit of her stomach that she realised that the usual icy chill had finally dispersed.

'You from Social Services?' demanded the woman next door, eyeing Jane's suit and briefcase with suspicion.

'What?' Already trembling on the edge of breaking down, the hostility brought tears to Jane's eyes. 'No. No. I work over there. At Euro-Freight.'

'What you want to know about Kylie for, then?'

'I used to talk to her on my way to work. I just wondered...'

The woman softened. 'Terrible business. I still blame myself. All that crying and her Mam never there. She was out when the fire started. Went up like a bonfire, it did. Proper inferno. We couldn't do nothing. And by the time the fire fighters got here, it was too late. Poor little mite didn't stand a chance.'

'My God!' breathed Jane. 'You mean she's dead? Kylie's dead?'

'Here, you all right? You'd better sit down before you fall down.'

Jane found herself perched on the edge of a sofa, her shaking hands clutching a mug of strong tea. The woman's voice seemed to be coming from a very long way away.

'They haven't done a thing to the place since, neither. I said to my sister, I said, fire or no fire, fancy leaving it empty all this time when there's families been on the council waiting list for years. Ent right, is it. Well, Dot, she says...'

'Just a minute,' Jane interrupted, confused, 'What do you mean all this time? When was the fire?'

'When? Last April. No, tell a lie, it must have been May. That's right. Yes. You know what? It must have been exactly a year yesterday, because our Gladys went into hospital that Tuesday for her veins...'

'But...'

'An' I'll tell you something for nothing. The day it happened was the first time I seen that kid smile. She was sitting out there on the grass playing with some doll and chattering away to herself for hours. I'd never seen her so happy, poor little mite.'

92

I'll Give Her Ghosts!
By Kathryn Brennan

Every legend has a remnant of truth, and the village of Mortunville has more than its fair share of tall tales, curses and legends. Mortunville is an ancient village (its original Latin name mortuus villa meaning village of the dead) and is built on a supposed ancient Roman burial site. Within its geography are many interwoven ley lines and powerful fields of energy; the effects of which make the present incumbents a very superstitious lot, especially at the festival of Hallowe'en.

It was one such day that seemed to be more than living up to the expectations of the villagers, this particular October 31st started with a gruesome discovery.

'Ghosts! I'll give her ghosts!' Ellen Bradley spat as she stomped down the path, out of her garden gate and headed towards the village, grumbling as she mulled over the events of earlier that morning. It was no ordinary day in Mortunville, it was the festival of Hallowe'en; a day when the village as a whole entered into the spirit of things celebrating the lives and deaths of previous residents. This particular festival had already got off on the wrong foot.

Ellen had not even dressed before there was a loud knocking at her door. She opened the door on the chain and was about to ascertain who was calling at such an early hour when she heard a familiar voice.

'Oh for goodness sake Ellen, let me in.'

Cora Stanbridge had almost forced the chain from its fixtures in her haste to gain entry to Ellen's house; once inside she stood staring at her with a look of what can only be described as expectant smugness on her face.

'Cora it's barely past seven. It's still dark.'

'Well yes, you see I couldn't wait any longer.' She said gleefully, 'Ellen it's happened, on today of all days!'

Ellen protested by tugging suggestively on the sleeve of her dressing gown indicating that she would still like some privacy but Cora had already marched in the kitchen, taken off her hat, coat and gloves and had settled herself down at the kitchen table before Ellen had realised that she was reasoning only with herself.

'So what is so thrilling that you have to get me out of bed in the middle of the night to tell me?'

'Oh for goodness sake Ellen, it's hardly the wee small hours, you were already up; your light was on and what I have to tell you can't wait.'

Ellen sat down opposite her at the table and stifled a yawn. After a long atmospheric pause Cora began to report her news.

'I woke early this morning, there had been a howling wind last night and I could see the shadow of the trees bowing across my window. I lay in bed for a while, the branches tapping on the glass as if they were trying to stop me from dropping back off to sleep. I knew something wasn't quite right and I felt myself drawn towards the window. I drew back the curtains slightly, the fog was very thick and for a few minutes I could see nothing but the orange hazy glow of the streetlamps. But then, very suddenly the fog lifted and the full moon shone through lighting up the lane and I could see across to Thorogood Hall; that's when I saw them.'

She waited again to build the atmosphere a little more, with Ellen hanging on her every word.

'There was a policeman at the bottom of the driveway to the house sealing it off with blue and white tape, and another one standing outside the main entrance to the Hall.'

Cora leaned closer to Ellen and continued in a low whisper drawing her further into her web of intrigue.

'I watched all the commotion for at least an hour. There were men going in and out of the house; some were even dressed in white overalls, they can only have been detectives of some sort.'

Ellen sat up abruptly 'What were they there for, is Mr Harris alright?'

'No Ellen. He's dead.'

'How do you know that?'

'Well put it this way, they wheeled him out on a stretcher in a body bag just over fifteen minutes ago.'

Ellen's eyes widened in surprise and she shook her head in disbelief. She rose from her chair and went to fill the kettle 'How do you know it was Mr Harris? It could have been anyone; there could have been an accident or a burglary that went wrong.'

'I know it was Mr Harris. I have just seen Peter Edwards the milkman, he found him.'

Ellen broke off from tea making and stood in thoughtful reflection for a moment.

'Poor Mr Harris, he's not lived here for very long. It's such a shame. All he wanted was a happy retirement here in the village.'

Cora rolled her eyes knowingly 'Well, he could have had a happy retirement, if only he had listened to us.'

'Listened to you?'

'I for one told him, and Peter Edwards did too; but oh no, he was a non-believer. It's always the case with outsiders thinking that they know best.'

Ellen abandoned the refreshments and sat down at the table again, 'Cora, what on earth are you talking about?'

'It's only the new folk in the village that ignore our customs and beliefs.'

'What do you mean, ignoring our customs and beliefs?'

'There is no doubt in my mind; James Harris was a victim of the curse.'

Ellen stared at her for a second or two trying to decide whether she was joking or if she really did believe the barmy nonsense spilling out of her mouth. Ellen scanned the self-satisfied look of defiance on Cora's face and came to the conclusion that she did indeed believe her own hype.

'Really Cora, that's too much. Mr Harris is dead and all you can do is whip up a storm of hocus-pocus and superstition.'

'You can mock if you like, but I know different. James Harris was killed by the ghost of Sir Oswald le Thorogood because he did not heed the ancient prophecy and leave the gate open to the graveyard on the night before All Hallows Eve', she declared triumphantly.

Ellen gave her a look of sheer bemusement.

'You might have lived in this village for over twenty five years Ellen, but unless you are born here you can never really understand the traditions that have made this village what it is and this includes taking very seriously the curse of Thorogood Hall.'

'Mortunville was founded by the wealthy Sir Oswald le Thorogood in 1465; he was a very powerful, yet decent man who cared about the village and its people. Sir Oswald was married to Isabella and they had a very precious son Edward. When Edward was five years old he caught a fever and died in his mother's arms. Both Isabella and Oswald were distraught at losing their only child; Isabella took it particularly to heart. On the first anniversary of Edward's death, October 31st1470, unable to bear the loss of her child, Isabella threw herself from the roof of Thorogood Hall. Oswald was mad with grief for the loss of his beloved wife and buried her with Edward in the graveyard next to the Hall. Every night before Hallowe'en he would go and stand by their grave hoping that his wife and child would come back to earth on the day they left the realm of the living, to visit him once more. Oswald pined away for Isabella and Edward, and within five years he himself was dead. His dying wish was that the gate to the graveyard be left unlocked every night before Hallowe'en so that he could visit their graves as he did in life, in the hope that Isabella and Edward may return to earth in search of him. It is said that his low mournful sobs can still be heard every night before All Hallows Eve as he searches for the long lost spirits of his wife and child. Anyone who fails to unlock that gate will suffer a terrible fate.'

Ellen's brow was furrowed as she gave her friend a look of sheer disdain 'You should be ashamed of yourself Cora, that poor man not yet cold and all you can do is peddle silly schoolyard stories. I know that you have had a lot of involvement in the organizing of this year's Hallowe'en festivities but if this is your idea of drumming up interest, I think it is rather poor. I'm sure the village will turn out in force anyway.'

Cora's face was red with anger 'Do you think I have made all this up just to get a better turn out tonight? Well I...'

Ellen cut her off, 'It's just far too convenient don't you think?'

Nostrils flaring with fury, taking great huffing breaths of air, Cora prepared to fight for her honour. She opened her mouth to retaliate when the sound of tuneless whistling and the chinking noise of glass milk bottles banging together made her pause and look towards the back door. She ran and seized the door handle and opened it with such force that a shocked Peter Edwards froze on the spot bending over the doorstep; only his eyes moved upwards to see what was coming towards him with such ferocity. When his brain registered it was Cora standing before him and not some demonic beast, he straightened up and clasped his hand to his heart.

'For goodness sake Cora, I nearly ended up the same way as old Mr Harris then! What's to do?'

'Mr Harris is to do', she turned around and shot a glare at Ellen who was looking at her in grim defiance.

Cora jabbed a finger in Ellen's direction 'I want you to tell her what's happened to Mr Harris.'

'Well he's dead!', said Peter, putting down his small crate of milk bottles. He leant against the wall, making himself comfortable before he began to tell all to his captive audience.

'The fog was so thick this morning that you couldn't see the hand in front of your face. It was so dark along the path that I drove around to the front of the Hall and parked the float at the bottom of the driveway and walked up. I thought there would be less of a chance of me falling over and doing myself a mischief.' He shook his head, 'Something just didn't seem right this morning. You know when you have that gut feeling in your stomach, that deep sense of foreboding? Well, I had that this morning and it wasn't until I got to the top of the driveway that I saw the gate to the graveyard was closed. I went to open it but it was locked.' He shivered as though someone had just walked over his grave. 'I carried on up to the house and I walked past the library window, the curtains had been drawn but I could see that the light was on. Not wanting to be nosey I walked past and put Mr Harris's milk on the doorstep.'

Cora nodded her head, urging him eagerly on with his tale.

'As I walked back past the library I noticed that the curtains were not actually drawn together properly and there was a break in them. I don't know what made me do it, but I tried to look through and I saw him, right there in front of me.' Peter screwed up his eyes and shook his head slowly trying to rid himself of the vision in his mind's eye. 'It was horrible, just horrible. James Harris was sitting sprawled in his chair his face contorted and almost unrecognisable, a look of sheer terror on his face.'

The sharp tone of Ellen's voice cut through the air, 'Is that the best you can do?'

Peter and Cora simultaneously turned to look at Ellen whose eyes were burning with fury. 'James Harris no doubt passed away because of a heart attack which would explain his facial expression.'

'I don't doubt that', exclaimed Peter 'I think I would have had a heart attack if Sir Oswald le Thorogood had come back to haunt me!'

Ellen shrugged her shoulders, 'There you have admitted it yourself, he probably had a heart attack.'

'But the gate to the graveyard was locked!', Peter tried to impress upon her.

'So he locked the gate to the graveyard; anyone would have done the same.'

'But it was the night before Hallowe'en, Ellen.', Cora said slowly, making sure that Ellen understood the implications.

'Why do you persist in believing stupid superstitions? There is no such thing as ghosts.'

Cora smiled at her but there was no warmth in the smile. 'It must be difficult for you to understand Ellen, you not actually having been born here, that the realms of the living and the dead exist in close proximity. We native Mortunvillians never underestimate the power of the spirit world.'

Cora walked over to the kitchen table and put on her hat, coat and gloves and walked back to the kitchen door before turning to face Ellen. 'Well, I have work to do if I am to be ready for tonight's ceremony. Even as a non-believer Ellen', she said huffily 'I do hope that you will still attend.' And with that declaration she turned briskly on her heels and marched from the house.

Peter gave Ellen a sympathetic look, she was not sure whether he was sorry for the upset caused between friends or whether he was sorry for her because she didn't believe. He picked up the milk from her doorstep and handed it to her before walking away after Cora. Ellen stood at the door listening to the sound of his whistling as he disappeared into the swirling dense fog.

Ellen shook herself trying to get rid of the upset of that morning, still angry at the two of them for their lack of sympathy. Even as a non-believer, as Cora put it, she was going to do her bit on All Hallows Eve. She was on her way to dress the Mortuus Apple tree, an ancient crab-apple tree

101

reputed to be centuries old and revered by the druids. They paid homage to this aged tree for its offering of mistletoe which was used in rituals to the gods, and also the harvest of crab-apples which they believed to be the food of the dead. Ellen had gathered the ivy and other woodland offerings the day before and packed them up ready to dress the centrepiece of the festival. There the celebration of the day would culminate in a moonlit ceremony where the spirits of the gods and goddesses would be invoked, bestowing their good grace upon the village for another year. As Ellen approached Thorogood Hall she noted that all that was left of the drama of the morning was a little piece of blue police cordon tape flapping in the stiff icy breeze. As she watched it dance in the air she noticed the figure of a woman standing on the drive.

Ellen stopped at the bottom of the driveway, and observed the woman a second before calling out to her. 'Are you alright there?'

The woman turned, smiled and began to walk towards her; she stopped so there was a short distance between them and looked back at the house without saying a word. Ellen took the measure of her, watching how the wind stirred the soft waves of her shoulder-length blonde hair. Even though she had only met James Harris on a few occasions she noted that the woman had the same pale blue eyes, the same bridge of the nose and the same square jaw, although it was slightly softer.

'Did you know Mr. Harris?', Ellen enquired, hoping to confirm her deductions.

The woman turned and smiled, 'Yes I'm his daughter, Lucy.'

Ellen introduced herself.

'I'm sorry, it must have been a great shock for you. Have you come far?'

The woman smiled, 'Far enough.'

Ellen nodded sympathetically 'Did you come on your own?'

'Yes.'

'You have no family at all with you?'

'No, they will come later.'

'And under such distressing circumstances too.'

The woman smiled at her again.

Ellen, not wanting to intrude too much on the woman's grief, offered her condolences one more time and said goodbye. She turned to watch her walk back up the drive to the house.

Ellen finally arrived at the apple tree and paused to take in the atmosphere. The tree was a mass of gnarled branches and was so old it was leaning at an angle almost trying to shelter itself within the leafless canopy of the other taller trees. She could feel the vibrations of energy and it was easy to understand why people worshipped this healing tree, so frail and wizened with age. The little bunches of dainty crab-apples ripened to yellow and red adorned it branches like jewels, their healing properties so renowned, powerful and awe-inspiring that people came to pay homage to the one true power, the power of Mother Earth. Within this atmosphere Ellen could hear the distant noise of centuries of song and music from the dancing rituals that took place around it on All Hallows Eve. She sensed the smell of smoke and burning herbs from the ceremonial fires and the food offered up to the god and goddess on feast days. This All Hallows Eve would be no exception.

After a few hours Ellen's work was done and she packed up her things and headed back home to prepare herself for the evening ahead. She approached Thorogood Hall once again and saw the woman still standing in the driveway. However, as she got closer she realised that it was a younger lady although the resemblance was there.

Ellen waved at her cheerfully and the lady responded in kind, walking down to greet her.

'I just came to see the house, I didn't get a chance before. My grandfather hadn't lived here for very long. I don't live locally; I should have come before but...'

Her voice trailed off.

Ellen patted her arm, 'There's no point in worrying now is there? Have you been here long?'

'No, I just arrived, I drove up this morning as soon as the Police telephoned.'

'That's such a shame, you probably missed her, I am sure she would have liked to have seen you.'

'Who would?'

'One of your relatives was here earlier.'

'One of my relatives? But who?'

'Mr Harris's daughter; Lucy.'

The wind had blushed the young lady's cheeks, but the colour suddenly drained from her face. 'I'm sorry, did you say Lucy?'

'Yes, I spoke to her myself. You look remarkably like her.'

'Are you sure she said her name was Lucy?', asked the woman, looking more perplexed.

'Yes dear, I spoke to her just like I am speaking to you. Why do you look so confused?'

'Lucy is my mother.'

Ellen smiled 'Yes I can see the resemblance.'

The woman didn't acknowledge the compliment. 'My mother died four years ago.'

Found At A Bedside
By Peter Stockwell

I am writing this in case something happens which may prevent me telling anyone personally. It is the story of events which were never expected. and which changed my life.

Living in a house such as mine is not always a conscious decision. If one buys a five hundred year old castle in Scotland complete with suits of armour, stags' heads and space for the framed lottery ticket, one might think that strange events go with the territory. But buying a Victorian farm house with a barn and a parcel of land is an everyday occurrence. I did not then believe in ghosts, apparitions, poltergeists or any other non-material phenomena, so such matters formed no part of the negotiations with the vendor.

The first sign of strange happenings was outside my bedroom door. I awoke one night to the sound of a heavy wooden block dropping onto floor boards and bouncing to rest. This was repeated several times and on several nights. In my newly-awakened state I rather accepted the matter until I remembered that the whole house was carpeted. I looked for rational explanations, plumbing, car doors outside, the natural movements of an old house cooling down at night. But actually it sounded just like a wooden block on a wooden floor.

One can get used to most things and the block in the night was infrequent and, whatever the reason, not particularly disturbing.

Then there was the episode of the bath towels. I had put a low and eminently stable pile of towels on a sofa ready to take upstairs. Going into the kitchen for a moment I returned to find them scattered the length of the sofa in a line as if they had been hit hard from one side. Just as if a cat had jumped onto them and skidded off. I did not, of course, have a cat. This was a worry, but then I had no belief in supernatural happenings. Perhaps the towels were not as stable as I had thought.

My niece came to stay for a week. So as not to alarm her, I made no mention of these events whilst she was visiting, but, en route to the airport, I casually admitted there had been a few strange things occurring, no doubt with a logical explanation.

'I knew it was haunted,' she said, 'I've been hearing footsteps going downstairs on wooden boarding but the stairs've got carpet.'

This was when, given the evidence, I began to wonder if the most logical explanation was that the house was indeed haunted.

Some time later I was writing in my study, the door began to rattle and shake as a fist banged on the upper panel.

'Go away,' I called out furiously, 'can't you give a chap a bit of peace!' It was at that moment I realised I had become a believer.

108

From that point onward, activity increased, lost things appearing, items changing position, unexplained noises. Nothing particularly harmful, more the activity of a naughty child. But my nerves were becoming frayed and I was sleeping badly.

They say that it is not a case of seeing is believing but more believing is seeing. I never saw the woman in the sitting room. My doctor thinks I did and that it triggered the next sequence of events, but I never actually saw her. I was aware of her.

A girl of about twenty five years of age, wearing a loose brown dress and with long brown hair, lying face down on the floor. One arm was raised and her cheek rested on the back of her hand. I just knew she was there. I took to rearranging my feet when I sat in the arm chair. It did not seem right to tread on her, besides there was no way of telling whether or not she was asleep.

The barn, older than the house, is Georgian. There was a period between the wars when it was used as a cart shed and then later it became part of a garage. The small man with a cap I saw there could have been a trick of the light, he was gone in an instant, leaving me unsure as to whether I had seen him at all. By this time however, I was becoming so agitated that even tricks of light were a setback. I was jumping at every noise and taking sleeping pills at night.

I had been speaking to my sister about these problems. A down-to-earth woman, she said what I needed was a few good meals and somebody to talk to. She would come and stay for a week to feed me up and get some sense into me. I was still working, although my performance was declining and I was being told to buck up my ideas. So Polly was left at home to relax, whilst I was at the office struggling to concentrate on matters of the day.

Returning home, I walked into the conservatory and glanced through a connecting door into the kitchen. Polly was standing at the table in a blue dress with her back to me.

'Hello Poll,' I called out, 'just dropping my things off. See you in a minute.' I walked back to the car, picked up my jacket and briefcase and, as I was going into the conservatory again, noticed my sister coming down the garden with an armful of flowers.

'You must have moved!' I said, admiring her turn of speed. 'You were in the kitchen a minute ago.'

She stared at me. 'Don't know where you got that fool idea, I've been picking flowers in the meadow until just now. I came down when I heard the car.'

I have never believed that one's hair stands up from shock, you know, really up on end, but I felt mine doing so.

'I saw you in the kitchen,' I said. 'It must have been a ghost.'

Polly looked puzzled. 'Perhaps it was my ghost. Do we know that ghosts are always of dead people?'

My hands were shaking, child poltergeists were one thing, probably slightly better than real children, but now we had three ghosts including one of a living person. Next day I went again to my doctor. He listened carefully and referred me to a psychiatrist at the local hospital. I also considered speaking to our vicar but, as I had never supported his church, felt that any help might be half-hearted and would, undoubtedly, have strings attached. All of which could serve to make matters worse.

Time passes. I am now on extended sick leave from the office. The psychiatrist seems unable to consider the possibility that my house might actually be haunted and does nothing more than address my agitation as a disease in itself. If, as it is said, madness is a dis-ease of the mind, then with my mind clearly in a turmoil of dis-ease, the question begged...was I mad? I did speak to my vicar who sympathised with my fragile emotional condition and recommended prayer and regular churchgoing on Sundays.

My sister died unexpectedly after a brief illness. I have not seen her ghost again but I do spend a lot of time in bed with the curtains drawn. There are so many happenings now that I no longer bother to record them. Recently, I have been trying to keep more calm, I have found the poltergeists are particularly active when I am distressed.

I bought a dog for company, but sometimes he wakes and whines or barks in the night. Perhaps, like me, he has become a believer.

As I sit at my desk writing, I can hear loud noises and breaking glass downstairs in my sitting room. I shall go downstairs to investigate.

Talking In The Park
By Sue Moorcroft

I was thirteen, and adults never seemed to know how much of the child remained in me. Not much, if the mascara and platform shoes were anything to go by, but still. Thirteen. Not an adult.

Most days, it was my job to walk my dog through the local park. Tammie was a carin, a shaggy terrier the colour of wheat with a laughing face. In the way that dog-walkers do, we built up a circle of acquaintances amongst other dogs and their owners.

Tam, who had an inclination to be fussy about her friends, would indicate which dogs she considered bearable, and I'd chatter to their owners. I was good at chattering. Some days a forty-minute walk could take me two hours.

I often reported to my parents on the dog-owners I'd met, and as I rarely got to know their names I'd reference them to their dog: Petra's Master, The Lady with the Two Setters or Pal's Mistress. However, the human who came along with my favourite dog, Scott, had told me his name. It was Roy.

Scott was an impressive Great Dane, almost as tall as I was even when all four mammoth paws were planted on the ground. Something of a contrast to my stumpy terrier. Tammie, who came over all girly when there was a really big chap like Scott around, would prance under his formidable chest, flattening her ears and wagging her whole body, and Scott would lower his massive black velvet muzzle and blow kisses.

Roy was a middle-aged man, dark hair, bright blue eyes, and a quick, nervous manner. He smoked tiny roll-up cigarettes. He originated from London and had the accent.

''Ello, Sausage,' he'd call. 'When you going to get a full size dog?' And he'd cackle with laughter as he strode on, relying on Scott to end his flirtation with Tam and lope after him like a small, thoroughbred horse floating over the grass.

One spring day, Tam and I were walking at the edge of the park by the brook, breathing in the soap scent of hawthorns and keeping away from the young green nettles.

Tam paused. She looked thoughtful, her ears pricked. The tip of her tail began to quiver like a rattlesnake's as she concentrated hard on a clump of bushes and trees ahead.

And, after a moment, Scott and his owner strode into view, Scott with his usual floating gait, Roy smoking a roll-up.

''Ello, Sausage,' he called. 'I see your dog ain't growed much!'

Tam and Scott embarked on their usual snuffling courtship and Roy and I chatted about how it was nice it was to see a bit of sunshine, and wasn't all that creamy blossom beautiful?

I remember that he seemed unusually cheerful and friendly. He wasn't normally one to stop for a prolonged chat, but that day he was sociable. His eyes were brighter than ever and he seemed unable to stop smiling, almost as if he were hugging a secret. We talked about the children enjoying themselves on the swings nearby and a game of football the older lads were organising on the flat bit of the park near the farmer's field.

Eventually, he stirred. 'Well, time's up, we better go, Scotty, hadn't we?' Scott looked up, and thrashed his tail.

I jingled Tammie's lead at her, ready to finish the circuit of the park. 'See you again.'

He paused, looked back. 'No, you won't, Sausage, to be truthful. I'm going away, and you won't see me no more.'

I supposed he was going back to London because he liked it better there. It probably explained his air of suppressed excitement.

I went on to pass the time with some of the girls watching the football match, and it was a couple of hours later that I met Pal's Mistress at the foot of the concrete alley leading to the road. She was walking with another woman and a dog called Sassy. Pal was a happy old black Labrador and Sassy was a brown dog of no discernible heritage, and both were on Tam's list of desirables, so we stopped again.

I told the women about seeing Scott and his owner, and how it was the first time I'd come across them for a few weeks.

115

'Not that man, dear,' Pal's Mistress contradicted, looking down the park, her white hair blowing in the wind.

I blinked. 'Yes, it was. He was with Scott, his name's Roy, and he stopped for a chat.'

Pal's Mistress pursed her lips. 'Not *Roy*! I can tell you you're mistaken, dear! I know him, and it couldn't have been him.'

I let it go. What was the point of arguing with adults once they decided to dictate to you as if you were a child? Adults could be like that. Sometimes they made a statement and it was *right*, and that was an end to it.

Even if it was wrong.

Even if I knew I'd been speaking to Roy and Scott, just as certainly as I was now talking to Pal's Mistress.

I shrugged, and went home.

I wasn't the only one to take Tammie out. My parents liked to stroll when they had time, and you don't go for a walk and leave the dog at home, do you? So, a couple of days later, it was my parents who took Tam out after dinner.

When they returned I was horizontal on the sofa, book in hand.

Tam raced in and threw herself in the air a couple of times in case I hadn't noticed that she was home, Mum put away the lead, and Dad dropped into his chair.

'We saw The Lady with the Two Setters, and Petra's Master,' he said. 'A Jack Russell tried to swap sniffs with Tam, but she saw him off.

'And we saw Pal's Mistress,' he added. 'She's a bit worried that she's said the wrong thing to you.'

I looked away from my book. 'Oh?'

'Apparently you were asking about Scott's owner the other day?'

'I mentioned him.'

Dad smiled, gently, he specialised in reassuring smiles. 'Unfortunately, darling, it seems the poor chap died. More than a week ago. Pal's Mistress had been to the funeral the day she saw you, and when you brought him into the conversation she was a bit flustered and didn't know what to say.'

'Roy's funeral?'

'That's what she said.'

I stared. 'If she was at his funeral, why couldn't she have just told me?'

He reached for his paper. 'Because some people are funny about discussing death with youngsters. She thought you might've burst into tears. So she told me instead, and asked me to pass it on.'

I thought. This must surely be nonsense. 'What about Scott?'

'He went to a neighbour. But he got out. They keep ringing the police about him, but he hasn't turned up.'

I went back to my book, thinking how sometimes grown-ups were just plain wrong, and wouldn't admit it. Pal's Mistress couldn't have been to Roy's funeral.

Could she?

And Roy couldn't be dead.

Could he?

Because I'd been talking to him in the park.

117

118

Oxford 16 Miles
By Jay Whitfield

'Me!'

'Yes, you *are* Miss Marianne James.'

I could hardly believe it. £100 would be nice, £1,000 would be fantastic – but to be left a cottage, a picturesque old stone cottage in the country – I was stunned. It's a brave girl who argues with an elderly solicitor in a dark suit with half moon glasses perched on the end of his nose.

'But,' I stammered, 'why me? Was my aunt…er sane?'

'I can assure you,' he said frostily, 'Miss Beatrice James was of sound mind and although in poor health was perfectly aware of her wishes.'

'I'd better go over there.' I got up and went to the door.

'Marianne, you need the key.'

'Oh yes…Thank you Mr Christie,' It was large and heavy, I was still in shock.

I checked the route to Hazlebury Martin. It had been a long time, but, as I entered the village, I somehow knew where to go. I turned right and drove up the grassy track we had run along as children. There it was, Glebe Farmhouse, with its lovely old Cotswold stone glowing golden in the afternoon sun.

119

It was a hot day in June, midges swarmed and old fashioned pink roses clambering up the walls, drooped in the heat.

'This is yours Mary, all yours.' I said out loud, looking round, using the name I'm always known by. They used to call me Marian...ny and I hated it.

The stone-flagged kitchen with the huge fireplace was as I remembered it from childhood, and five minutes later, as I sipped icy cold water, I knew why we had stopped coming here as children.

I tiptoed through the rooms. From the kitchen a scullery lead out to the yard and an outside toilet. In the parlour was an elegant chaise longue in faded red brocade, with a folded duvet and pillow laid over it. All was tidy and I got the impression that that was where Aunt had been sleeping. Was she too frail to go upstairs?

I climbed up the wooden staircase, buffed smooth by centuries of feet. I opened doors and peeped in. The bedrooms were cool and calm. Wood was polished, the covers were clean and windows sparkled. The bathroom had the bare essentials and a cold black and white tiled floor. It made me shiver looking at it.

As I entered the kitchen, flicking a cardigan round my shoulders I was surprised to see a man standing by the fireplace.

'Oh! Hello,' the ticking clock was the only sound and he just stood looking at me, smiling.

'Mary you've come back. It's been a long time.' He was middle-aged, with long grey hair tied back in a ponytail. His white shirt with baggy sleeves was a bit quaint, but he could have bought it in London.

'Well, yes it has been quite a while since we were here.' Twenty years at least. 'I'm not sure if I'm staying, this is a…huge shock.'

'Oh my dear, you had a terrible shock, how I've grieved for you.'

I stared, it wasn't a nasty shock, just unexpected. Perhaps we had out wires crossed? I wasn't really grieving for my aunt, I hadn't even gone to her funeral.

'Did you know Aunt Beatrice well?' The tingly ring of my mobile interrupted us. I reached for it murmuring, 'Excuse me.' and walked to the window.

Paul, my husband sounded so close, 'Are you all right sweetheart? How's it going?'

'Well you'd never guess, but I'd better ring you back, I have a visitor.' And I turned, but he had gone. 'Oh, that's funny, there was this middle-aged guy standing in here and he knew my name.'

'Where are you?'

'Paul, Aunt Beatrice has left me her cottage. We have our very own country cottage, complete with…well, not really complete because there's no electricity and no telephone. No wonder we stopped coming here, you know how my mother likes her modern conveniences.' I laughed, 'There's freezing cold water in the scullery and I think my aunt was living downstairs.'

'Mary, when are you coming home?'

'I'll stay here tonight, I'll sleep in the parlour and I'll grab a meal in the pub. I'll have to light candles like we used to do. I can't believe this.'

'Who was this man you said was there?'

'I don't know, he must be a neighbour and saw the car.'

'Keep your phone with you, I suppose you can't charge it if there's no electric.'

'I'll ask at the pub for that, I'm going to have a look round now, bye love.'

I slipped the phone in my skirt pocket and went from the cool house to the bright, hot garden. Bees droned, laden with pollen, beautiful blue dragonflies darted round my head and I saw a small pond covered with lilies and green algae. The lawn was mown and the flowerbed under the window was tidy with marigolds and borage. It felt like the garden was waiting for my aunt to come home. I lay on the grass and balled the cardigan up under my head. It had been a long drive, I was tired and as I drifted off to sleep I heard the sound of children's laughter.

There was crying, and my mother saying, 'Give her a chance, let Mary have a turn. Alex don't do that.'

I woke with a start. I had lain out in the hot sun and my head was pounding. I shifted to the silver birch tree and leant against the trunk and watched as a small middle- aged woman in a print dress came round the corner.

She came across the grass, 'Afternoon,' was in a broad Oxfordshire dialect.

'Hello.'

'I'm Anne James. I sees the car, I been expecting you.' Another one!

'I've only just found out today about my aunt's will.'

'I knew her well, I looked after her, she told me about you.'

'You kept the house clean, and ', I waved an arm, 'mowed the grass.'

'Aye, I said I would. You'll be staying then?'

'Well only for today, I haven't got any plans.'

'Oh you must stay, she wanted you to. It's Midsummer Day tomorrow, there's a fayre coming. We'll all be there.'

I smiled to take away any implied criticism. 'Mrs James, there's no electricity here. I need to boil a kettle, have a bath and well… I've got no clothes with me.'

'I'll light the wood burner in the kitchen, you can boil a kettle on that, it soon heats up. Miss James used to put her saucepans on that. I says to her, why don't you get the electric on, you could have a telly – but she says no, she wants to keep it natural, for when they come back.' She turned. 'I'll bring you some food up from the shop.'

'Oh, by the way, there was a man here earlier – he seemed to know me. And who's they?', but she had gone.

With long white candles in old pewter candlesticks and the wood burner glowing it was cosy in the kitchen that evening. I had promised to stay.

Another cloudless summer day gave us dry throats at the fayre in the field near my cottage. People were guardedly friendly, but I was an outsider. I bought a cake for my tea and decided to go home after breakfast the next day. I wished Paul was with me, without him I felt incomplete and unsettled and I wandered alone back to the cottage.

The kitchen was chill without the stove and I lit it and fetched in logs. I could imagine the novelty of that wearing off quite rapidly. Later I felt tired after all the fresh air and decided to lie on the chaise and talk to Paul. I stepped back into the kitchen cursing because I had to light the candles again and shook my head in disbelief. Standing by the fireplace was a woman in a long dark dress with a white apron and a white bonnet.

'Oh my God,' I whispered, 'the place is haunted.' I watched her glide to the door and disappear through it. Just like they do in films. I ran to it, wrenched it open and looked. She sort of shimmered across the yard and up the lane turning right by the pub. No one was about and feeling brave, I followed, keeping my distance. It was cool and dark under the trees as I followed her up a narrow lane. Sheep were bleating in the field behind the hedge.

Suddenly there was the thundering of horses' hooves, a voice was yelling and I felt a terrible thump on my back. Horses were neighing and voices shouted. I pitched headlong into the ditch sprawling in brambles and nettles, hitting my head on a slab of old stone. I struggled to pull myself up and gingerly felt my head for a lump. Brambles tore at my skirt and legs and with a shaking finger I traced the inscription on the stone that said OXFORD 16 MILES.

I sat up feeling ridiculous. I was sitting on the verge of the A 426 with cars whizzing by. I blinked, where was the lane, where was the ghost? I felt wet trickling down my face and tasted blood. Hurriedly I smoothed down my skirt and jogged back to the village feeling dishevelled and foolish as I scurried past the pub. When I reached my open door I saw the candles flicker and a shadow pass and I began to feel very frightened. I turned to go and sit in my car and Ann James was right behind me.

I shrieked, 'What are you doing creeping up like that?'

'I've brought you some eggs and bacon for the morning.' She peered up at me. 'Have you had an accident?'

I put the kettle on to boil and shuddered as I sat in the old Windsor chair.

'I think I saw a ghost, I followed it, I had a fall up the road.'

'That's Mary James, killed in 1801 she were, up on the Oxford road, looking for her son. Went out of here, this very room and never came back.'

'Oh my God,' I closed my eyes. 'What day was it?'

'Midsummer Eve. And there was a lodger here at the time, Robert Southwell. They say he'd fallen in love with her. Miss Beatrice reckoned he's still waiting for her to come back, waiting for his Mary. All her life she looked for them, even slept down here, she did. And you sees them both, just like that. Chosen you are, you'll have to stay.'

'Oh no, I'm going home tomorrow.' But she had gone and the grey haired man stood in the doorway, holding his hand out to me.

'You're a ghost, a shadow, I refuse to believe in this.' I was terrified and I screamed. 'I'm walking out of here, try and stop me.'

Trembling, I grabbed my bag and checked the candles were safe. No way was I going to leave in total darkness. He was by the fireplace when I got to the door. I had a splitting headache from the fall and, in a foul temper I slumped onto my car seat but when I turned the ignition nothing happened, the battery was dead.

'No, no', I moaned, tears streaming down my face. 'It can't be. Go, damn you, go.' Nothing happened, not a sound.

'I'll phone Paul,' I whispered, I thought the man could hear me, even see me. I punched in the numbers and it came up Out of Time. I swore softly, every single word I could think of.

I checked my doors were locked and turned on the radio. I listened to Classic FM for hours, Schubert, Chopin, Mozart went through in a quiet stream of sound. I hunched down and peeped over the steering wheel. A shadow seemed to pass in front of the cottage window and I said, 'Jesus, he's still there, don't ghosts ever rest.'

I dozed in the early hours of dawn and awoke with a start when I smelt burning. Horrified I watched my cottage blaze. Smoke poured through the thatch and hungry flames licked around rotten wooden window frames. I gazed on and on mesmerised. There was nothing I could do or wanted to. Once I saw the shadow again.

Then I heard the scream of sirens and people were there. Someone knocked on the window and I wound it down.

'You all right miss?' It was an elderly policeman.

'Yes, thank you.'

'Why, it's Miss James, spitting image you are.'

'Image of who?'

'Your grandfather dear, it's the hair…and the nose.'

I heard a shrill voice, 'She did it, she don't want the cottage. Stop her, arrest her, she's…she's killed 'em all.' Ann James, inciting the villagers, was purple-faced with fury.

Later that morning, in the smoking, stinking, charred remains they found a misshapen pewter candleholder and a pool of wax.

Two and two made a short prison sentence. It seemed that half the village, whose surname was James, were prepared to testify that I had bought paraffin in the shop. Paul and I don't go within fifty miles of the place now.

I have paid the price and worn the tee-shirt and I flung the key in the ditch by the milestone.

Lucy
By Elizabeth Crooks

When my husband was serving in the R.A.F. we returned to England homeless, from an overseas tour. We were housed on a new housing complex that had been built on the site of a small wood at the rear of the Abbey in Cirencester. It was a pleasant site and a nice little house in the middle of a terrace.

However, one day soon after moving in I heard footsteps following me as I descended the stairs. The hair on the back of my neck stood up as I knew I was alone in the house. Curiosity got the better of me and I turned at the bottom to see who it was. There halfway down was a young girl, a teenager and a stranger to me. I had goose-pimples all over as I met her gaze.

She was dressed fifties style in a yellow blouse, cream circular skirt, flat black pumps and white ankle socks. Around her neck was a small scarf knotted at one side, her black hair was cut in a bob with a side parting and she wore no make-up on her smooth fresh face. I stared at her stupefied and speechless; she smiled at me, an open smile showing even white teeth. Just as I was recovering and about to speak, she disappeared into thin air.

I was shocked, I can tell you and in need of a cup of tea. Then I began to feel a bit scared to venture into the hall or go up the stairs. However life must go on, I had children to collect from school but after that I did make an effort to put it to the back of my mind. I convinced myself I had imagined her.

Some weeks later I had reason to visit a part of the town new to me. My eldest son was intent on joining the Cubs and Mrs. Barnes who worked in the café-cum-bakery gave me the address of Akela. It took me best part of the morning to find the house and luckily Akela was at home. On hearing my request the lady asked me in for a cup of tea while she took down my son's details. It had been a long walk and I was glad of the rest.

Directing me into the lounge Akela went to put on the kettle. It was a pleasant sunny room and I went to sit on a dining chair placed by the sideboard. My blood ran cold and my hair stood on end, spiked out at the back of my neck as I gazed at the photo of a familiar face. It was in a large silver frame in the centre of the sideboard and she stood at the front door of this house dressed exactly as I had seen her in my house. As it was a black and white photo I had no way of knowing the colour of her clothing but I was in no doubt it was the same girl.

When Akela returned I plucked up courage and said. 'What a lovely girl,' as I pointed to the picture. 'Yes, my late sister,' she replied. I pressed on, feeling extremely rude, but my curiosity was getting the upper hand. 'Was she wearing a yellow top and cream skirt that day?' I knew I was being intrusive but I couldn't seem to help it. 'Yes, but as I say she is no longer with us. It was sad and that photo was taken the day she died.' I could feel the pain in her voice and was unable to go on so, as soon as she had the required details, I left.

On the way home questions crowded my mind; how had she died? Was it an accident? She certainly looked the picture of health in the photo and in my house five weeks ago. So, after picking up my youngest from nursery school at lunch time, I decided to treat us both to lunch at the 'Copper Kettle'. Mrs. Barnes was on duty, 'Good,' I thought as we took our seats. It was quiet in the café and I was able to engage the lady in conversation. 'Thank you for your help with the Cubs, I've been to see Akela this morning,' I began, before launching into the questions I wanted answers to.

'What about that sister of hers, she died very young didn't she?' Mrs. Barnes prided herself at knowing everything that went on locally and rose to the bait, telling me. 'Well, it was twenty years ago, and she was murdered in the very copse where the houses you live in are built.' She folded her arms under her ample bosom and paused noting my shocked reaction before going on. 'Yes a lovely young girl like that, Lucy her name was, she took a short cut through that little wood once too often. It was in all the papers when she went missing.' Mrs. Barnes was enjoying this, 'Four days the police searched that area before they found her, strangled, she was. Strangled with that scarf she wore.'

'What colour was the scarf?' I couldn't resist asking.

'Why yellow and white, spotted I think.'

131

'Everyone wore them to match their outfits in the fifties,' I added lamely as she peered suspiciously at me thinking no doubt that I had taken leave of my senses. 'Yes a yellow blouse and cream skirt, or was it the other way round. Yellow would be her colour with the dark hair.' Mrs. Barnes mused. I knew I was pushing my luck but I ploughed on. 'Did they catch the one who did it?'

'No, the murderer was never caught and people stopped using it for a short cut. So it became overgrown and eventually, like I say, those houses was built there.'

Some weeks later we were moved again and I never gave Lucy another thought. That is until years later when I saw a report in the paper about the arrest of an old man for the murder of a young girl. She was strangled in the area of Cirencester where we had lived. She was wearing a scarf knotted around the neck; the style had been revived from the fifties it seems. While he was being interrogated by the police he confessed to the murder of two other girls. One of them was Lucy.

Why Lucy visited me that day I will never know, I wish I had been able to help her but I hope she is at peace now that her murderer is behind bars.

Little Chapel Wedding
By Kathleen Croft

I had got quite friendly with my new neighbour Janice and had helped her unpack the smaller boxes of belongings after she had moved in. That was when she told me she had no relatives, just an ex. In fact it was only a week last Wednesday that we'd emptied the last cardboard box, mainly junk and a couple of old books.

'Why do you want these old books? They're a bit past it aren't they?'

'They were my granddad's and they remind me of him; make me feel secure.'

We soon established a routine of morning coffee and an afternoon walk, supposedly to collect the kids from school. We could easily have taken turns but we enjoyed each other's company and the walk got us out of the house for half an hour, so what was the harm? It wasn't as though we had anything more pressing to do, unless of course you call the ironing a pressing job. As a single parent Janice had need of company and my husband works away from home for long periods, so we both had a lot to gain from a good friendship. It was on one of these afternoon excursions that she suddenly said,

'You know last weekend when I took the kids to Wales to visit their dad?'

'Yeah'

'I saw my grandparents' wedding.'

'Your grandparents' wedding? Don't be daft, you couldn't go to their wedding? Anyway I thought you said they'd died?'

'They are; have, I mean. Three years ago.'

'Well then, you couldn't go to their wedding.'

'I didn't say I went to their wedding. I said, I saw their wedding.'

I stopped and stared at her, she was clearly upset.

'OK you'd best tell me all about it and I'll try not to interrupt you again.'

She was silent for awhile, and then very softly she told me this weird story.

'You know that because of Darren's nightshift starting this week, I stopped over and brought the kids back myself; to save Darren the journey up and down on Sunday evening.'

'Yes, you stayed in that little bed and breakfast on the Mumbles. The one Harry and I and the kids went to last year.'

'Well, on the Saturday morning I walked round the village, but there was nothing much open. The seaside doesn't have a lot going for it in late October. Anyway, after lunch it started to rain so I drove up into the hills and I came across a pretty little Chapel built into a hillside. I've no idea where I was; I'd travelled a long way. I could see a lady sweeping the steps, so I stopped the car to ask the way back, but before I could get out of the car she'd gone down some steps by the side of the building. I

134

don't know why but I followed her, by the time I got round the building and down the steps she'd disappeared. There was an open door and I could hear her feet echoing up the steps, so I ran after her and I found myself in a modernised multi-purpose chapel. There was a small pulpit to my right, with perhaps five or six rows of seats arranged in front of it. Extra chairs were propped up against the other wall; they looked like an alterative altar. Behind me, tight into the corner is the inside of the door where I had seen the lady sweeping; there was no sign of her in the room though. I sat down on one of the chairs in front of the pulpit. Oh Karen, I was so lonely. I think I still love Darren, why, oh why, did I leave him?'

'I know, I know,' I said, just trying to help her come to terms with the emotions that she was so obviously feeling. Loneliness is a killer; the need to communicate is strong in everyone. Sometimes anyone is better than no one at all. I know from my own loneliness, Harry being away from home so much; and I have family to help me. Janice has no one. Her father had done a runner after her mother died and she only had her grandparents and now they were gone. What must it be like, to be so alone and with children to bring up single-handed?

'I didn't hear the wedding party arrive.' Her quiet voice interrupted my thoughts. 'They came in so quietly. All I heard was a quiet cough, the rustle of a page being turned in a hymnbook and the shuffle of feet; they didn't seem to know I was there, and do you know what was even weirder? They stood in front of the stacked chairs, not the altar. I thought it was a themed wedding, you know what I mean, medieval with lots of green ivy or Edwardian with high stiff collars. Well, this was a nineteen-forty style wedding, not at all modern, no stretch limo, no designer dresses and it was so gentle. I've never seen a wedding like it. There were maybe, twenty guests, and the ladies were all wearing little hats, tilted forwards over one eye and their dresses were knee-length in a sort of flowery silk crepe-de-chine. And oh! You should have seen their shoes; Cuban heels, very heavy and sensible; they all wore white gloves and carried little pouch handbags.' Janice was not in the street with me, she was away in her memory.

'All the men wore dark pinstriped suits and had a spray of white heather in their buttonhole. I couldn't see a piano but I heard one playing the Wedding March. The bride came in wearing a dress of parachute silk; I knew it was parachute silk, my gran's wedding dress had been of parachute silk; I used to play dressing up in it as a child.' This memory of her gran seems to sadden her and she surreptitiously wipes away a tear. I pretend not to notice.

'The dress was so simple, just a slightly flared skirt, lightly gathered at the waist. The sweetheart neckline showed off the single string of pearls she wore around her neck; it was just perfect; exactly right. She moved slowly across the room and the groom stepped forward to greet her. And oh! Karen, her father kissed her fingers before he passed her hand to the groom. The whole service was so courteous, so much love.' She's silent now and I dare not make any comment, we arrive at the school and greet the children, we lovingly admire pictures and toilet-roll models; there's no further mention of the wedding.

It's Sunday before I learn any more, Harry is away until a week on Tuesday and of course Janice is alone as usual. We decide to take the kids to Brewster for a treat and while they play on the climbing frames we sit on hard chairs drinking cheap lager.

'Do you want to tell me more about the wedding?' I'm desperate to know more but I don't want to pressure her. 'If you don't want to talk about it just tell me to shut up.'

'No, it's all right, I don't mind you asking. I didn't want to bore you with it, you must think I've lost the plot.'

'Don't be stupid, why would I think that?'

'It was such a strange experience.'

'For heavens sake.' I'm impatient with her. 'I'm dying to know more. Were there any bridesmaids and what did they wear?' She smiles at me and I see the relief in her eyes.

'Just one bridesmaid, wearing a very shabby puff sleeved dress in turquoise taffeta. The skirt had a narrow band of ruche inset, just above the frilled hemline; it had been torn and was badly mended, big stitches of white cotton. She had these odd looking big clumpy black lace-up shoes; more like you would wear in winter; not at all nice for a wedding. I watched as best I could, but it was difficult to watch all the time. My neck began to ache and I turned away. It went very quiet, so I looked round and they

137

were leaving through the front door. I could see people throwing confetti and I heard them laughing and shouting 'good luck', 'be happy' and 'best wishes for a long and happy life together'. I thought, 'why am I not happy like them?' I sat a bit longer; I didn't want to be in the way as they took photographs. When I did go out they'd gone and Karen, I felt as though I had lost something important to me.' She stops talking and unsure of what to say I pat her hand. We sit in companionable silence for a while and then I go and buy another two half-glasses of the repugnant lager. We sip uninterestedly and watch the kids as they pluck up courage to come down the tube slide.

After a while she says, 'The lady had come back.'

'You were still on the steps outside?'

'Yes, she had come back for the brush and was about to go back inside when I said to her, 'It must be difficult, sweeping up the confetti.''

'Do they allow people to throw confetti these days Janice?'

'No they don't, that's what she said, so I told her that the wedding had thrown confetti, I'd just watched them do it. And she said 'What wedding?' 'The Forties themed wedding. Just now.' I said. 'Whilst I sat in the Chapel.' But she said there hadn't been a wedding. Themed or otherwise. 'Yes there was.' I told her. 'Just a few minutes ago.' She gave me a strange look and picked up the dustpan. I thought, 'I must be going mad; I have just seen a wedding I know I have'. It was getting dark and misty and I must have shivered in the damp air,

138

because she asked me, 'Are you all right? You look awfully pale.' But I couldn't answer. I tried to speak but instead I started to cry. She opened the heavy door and took me back inside, guiding me across the long room, through a door and into a kitchen; I sat at the wooden table, on a rickety chair whilst she made us tea. She was so kind Karen, and asked me to tell her all about it. I said, 'I must be going mad. I'm so sure I saw a wedding.' She said, 'Perhaps you got too warm, with your thick anorak on, dozed off and had a dream'. So I agreed with her, it seemed easiest, but I'm sure it wasn't a dream Karen, I'm positive I saw a wedding. But if I'd insisted, she would definitely have thought me mad and I was already having doubts about my sanity. The experience had disturbed me deeply.'

'It must have.' I couldn't help but think Janice must have been on some kind of happy juice.

'I needed to change the subject Karen; so I said to her, 'This part of the chapel seems quite new' and she said, 'Yes, it is. Well, no not new exactly.' Then she told me. 'Forty or fifty years ago, there was a fire and this upper floor was ruined. The church leaders decided it ought to be restored and raised the money by holding raffles, jumble sales, etc. Anyway, after it was done, they found it was too big for the size of the congregation; so it was divided and made into the big hall out there, this kitchen and a smaller meeting room. It's a community hall as well as a chapel now.' So I asked her 'Is that why the main door is not in the centre of the room?' 'Yes,' she said, 'and they moved the altar.' I said, 'Did it used to be where the chairs are stacked?' She didn't seem to know but said if I went back on Sunday for the service she would ask the older members of the congregation about it; she was sure they would know. I was still confused but I managed to get outside without making any more of a fool of myself.'

'You're not a fool.' I say, trying to cover my doubts about this story.

'So I went to the service.'

'You in a chapel?' I laughed. 'It's enough to make pigs fly.'

'Yes, I know.' She smiled at the memory of herself, sitting in a pew, singing hymns. Then she said 'I prayed as well. I meant my prayer too, so don't laugh. And they told me the altar used to be where the chairs were stacked.'

And wouldn't you just know it, as the tale is getting dramatic the kids decide to fall out and we have to make our way home.

'Janice, you must tell me the rest of the story tomorrow.'

'Well, that's basically all there is to tell.'

'So, how do you know it was your gran's wedding?'

'I'll show you tomorrow, when you come round for coffee.'

'Show me?'

'Yes, show you.'

I took ages to get to sleep, Janice's story went round and round in my head; it seemed too far-fetched to be true. She must have eaten hallucinatory mushrooms for breakfast that Saturday morning in Wales. I rushed through the washing and got it hung out on the line and then I was round at Janice's in quick sticks. Over coffee she showed me her photograph.

'That's the chapel.'

'Are you sure?'

'Of course I'm sure. See how it's built into the hillside and those steps there, they're the ones that lead down to where the side door is. That's where I went in, down there.'

'Whose wedding is this?'

'My grandparents. It has their names and the date pencilled on the back. It's very faint, I had to use granddad's magnifying glass to read it. They never talked about their wedding, so I've never known much about it or where they married.'

'Doesn't it say on the wedding certificate?'

'I suppose it must, if I could find it.'

'They look so happy.'

'Yes. My grandmother looks to be about twenty, maybe twenty-one, no older. But look at the bridesmaid.'

I look again at the black and white photo. The seated bridesmaid seems ill at ease in this formal setting. She is trying to hide her shoes beneath the hem of her dress but they show quite clearly; heavy lace ups and probably black, but of course on an old photo, they could be any dark colour, so we can't be sure. There is however a definite mend in the ruche on the front hemline of her dress.

'Are you sure you haven't imagined all this?' I ask her. 'After all you must have seen this photo many times before.'

141

'But that's the point. I found this photo inside one of those old books of grandad's, in that last box we emptied; the box you helped me to sort through a couple of weeks ago and I have never seen this photograph before in my life. I'm not sure what I experienced in that little chapel. Whether it was a memory of my grandparent's wedding I saw or whether I dreamt the whole thing I will never know. But I do know my grandparents loved each other completely and I feel that they were there, guiding me to make a better decision for my future. This experience has made me realise how much I still love Darren and that I should never have left him. So, I rang him last night to see if he feels the same and he does; the long and the short of all this is, I'm going back to Wales, to Darren.

Sickness Takes The Mind
By Jim Harwood

'Sickness can surely take the mind
Where minds can't usually go
Come on the Amazing Journey
And learn all you should know'
Pete Townshend – Tommy.

'I had an interesting experience last night', I said to whoever was sat at my bedside. The morphine, the antibiotics, the post-operative state, or the combination of all meant I couldn't trust my senses any more. There could have been a group of people there; there could have been one. I knew someone was there because they spoke from the real world.

'A dream, you mean?'

'No, not a dream, at least I don't think so. I was awake.'

'So what was it then?'

'What?'

'The interesting experience.'

'I'm about to tell you, but don't interrupt, please. Thinking is hard enough, let alone speaking.'

I tried to adjust my position by pressing down on the mattress and pushing myself up, but nothing was happening. My bedside companion moved to help.

143

'No, get me a nurse. Get two.'

An eternity later I was slightly more upright, gasping for air, seething with annoyance at my immobility, and I'd completely forgotten what I was doing. I reached for what I thought might be a glass of water, but it wasn't where I thought it was, and it wasn't a glass of water. I closed my eyes and remained thirsty, my throat hot and dry. There was a voice talking to me from the real world, but I couldn't hear it distinctly. My bed rippled constantly, to encourage circulation, a slight undulation, up, then down, up, then down. As the mattress rippled silently beneath me, so waves of sensation washed over me, from burning intense pain to tingling whispers of pleasure.

'Here you are, James, a nice cup of tea!', announced a loud voice in my ear.

Who was James? Must be me.

From wherever I'd been I was dragged back to the hospital ward with a sickening jolt. I gestured for my oxygen mask so I could breathe something cool, and slowly the ghouls drifted away and everything real swam back into focus.

I gulped the lukewarm, milky tea, and tried to think of something to say to my companion.

'Has everyone else gone?'

'Everyone else?'

'The others.'

'No-one here but me, buddy!'

'Ah.'

'You were telling me about an interesting experience…'

'Was I? I've had a few of those just recently, never a dull moment, ha ha.'

'Last night? You said it wasn't a dream, that you were awake?'

'Ah, yes!' I lifted up the trigger for the morphine drip, a grey tube with a red button on the end, a new innovation in 1994. 'With this little beauty, this somewhat drab, uninspiring place becomes a whole other world at night!'

...only last night was different. I was trying to lay off the morphine during daytime as I was getting a lot of visitors and wanted to be able to communicate, but, at night, when the last visitor had tiptoed away and the pain and the loneliness set in, I'd hit that button all the way to oblivion, a shortcut out of hell.

Last night though, something told me not to use it. I felt I needed to know just how much pain I was in. It was a lot. They say the memory cannot remember pain, and if it could, no words would be adequate to describe how I was feeling then.

I remember drifting in and out of consciousness quite regularly, and then I was suddenly clearly awake. The time was irrelevant. Nothing seemed different at first, and I just lay there staring into the gloom.

It wasn't until a dark figure walked, or rather glided, past the end of my bed that I began to realise that all was perhaps not as it should be. I clearly saw a large woman in a long dark dress with a large bustle, a white lace collar and a small white lacy hat. She just slid past and disappeared into the darkness. Then I noticed that the dim lights glimmering along the walls were gaslights, and I could hear them hissing faintly, and sometimes sputtering. The curtains round the beds no longer hung from rails, they were stretched between painted metal frames. There was no need to pinch myself, I was in enough pain already. I felt afraid, but my dad told me to settle down. I'd forgotten he was there. He helped me get out of bed, and with my small hand wrapped in his big rough fist, we walked slowly over to the window to watch the snow. I could smell his suit. Coal fires and warm beer. I was a small child seeing snow, not for the first time, but for the magical thing it was. I had to stand on tiptoe and I could smell the wood of the window frame, and hear the glass shivering. We were looking out of a ground floor window, across a main road, and our view looked down a street which was familiar to me. My dad stood outside looking in, looking out of place and cold. The snow was deep and heavy on the ground, with no footprints or tyre tracks. Big, thick snowflakes swirled around. I yawned, and my breath steamed up the window. My dad carried me back to bed, and just rested his hand on my head, like he'd done once when I'd sprained my ankle. I felt a warm healing power spread through me, easing and soothing and cooling the pain better than any drug, but I didn't sleep. When I looked again he'd gone. I could hear voices mumbling, but not what they were saying. My eyes focussed on a strip of incongruous light just beyond the foot of my bed. The toilet door stood ajar, and from within, the yellow glare of an electric light sliced through the darkness. Without understanding why, I knew that if I went through that door, when I came back out, everything would be as it should.

My legs felt unbearably hot. With great difficulty, I managed to ease myself out of the side of the bed, holding onto my drip hook for support, and I knelt on the floor to feel the cold of the linoleum on my skin. My head felt heavy, and the door through which I had to go seemed a long way off. I tried to stand but couldn't, and I rested my head on the edge of the bed and cried as silently as I could.

The woman in the long dark dress came to my side, but I couldn't hear what she was saying. Through my tears I managed to make her understand that I had to go into the toilet, and she helped me to my feet, and when I finally stood, they felt wrong. They'd swollen up from not being used for a week, and my bare soles felt as fat as tractor tyres. I wobbled for a bit, then I pushed her away, determined to make it to the light on my own, which I did by leaning heavily on my drip hook, and shuffling without actually lifting my feet off the floor. My head kept falling forwards until my chin pressed on my chest, and it was all I could do to lift it up to see where I was going. I stood beneath the electric light, my eyes stinging with tears. I looked down at the gleaming white bowl of the modern toilet, with its still pool of clear water, and knew that everything would be alright.

I turned slowly round, opened the door, and peered into the darkness of the ward. A nurse in a pale grey uniform was waiting for me.

147

'Come on now mister, back to bed. How on earth did you get all the way over here?'. Her black, shiny face creased in a wide grin, she led me back to bed, speaking softly the whole time. She had to get another nurse to help me back into bed, and together they checked my pulse and blood pressure, examined my drips, and asked me my name and date of birth.

'Use your morphine, it'll help you sleep, you're in a lotta pain.' I nodded as she took the thermometer from my mouth, pushed the red button with my thumb, and was gone.

When I awoke, the usual July sun was blazing through the sixth floor window of the brand new hospital wing.

'Interesting,' said my companion, whose existence I'd completely forgotten, 'Do you know where this other place was?'

'Well, I'm pretty certain it was on Regent Road, and we were looking down King Street. Back of the Bricklayers Arms, where the car park is.'

He looked alarmed at this, but said nothing.

It's impossible to find any kind of explanation or rationale. The night staff had noticed nothing unusual, but the nurse who had found me kneeling by the bed cooling my knees had thought I was praying, and laughed when I told her the more mundane reason. She did wonder at how I'd managed to get myself into the toilet when I was incapable of walking. At the time I was deeply traumatised. I had been stabbed, apparently. I had lain unconscious in Intensive Care for three days, during which time my heart had stopped beating for almost a minute. I had woken up on the operating table, my belly split open like a human canoe. I had a tramline of stitches holding me together from my chest to my groin. I was on drips for food, morphine and antibiotics, but my memory of this incident is as clear today as the night it happened, in every detail.

My friend came back to me a day or two later, and told me of the existence of a cottage hospital, which had stood on the very spot I had described. I was not surprised, as though it was something I'd known all along. The hospital had been demolished long before I came to Leicester, and I don't think there was any way I could have known. My Dad had died in 1973, and to the best of my knowledge had never been to Leicester in his life. When I saw him that night, it was the big, solid Dad I saw, not the thin wasted figure he became before he died.

The day before all this, my physiotherapist had reduced me and almost herself to tears in her efforts to get me out of bed and onto my feet and walking. The pain, in spite of the morphine and voltarol, was too much. The day after, I was able to walk unaided, and the morphine drip was removed. Hardly a miracle; it wasn't as if I'd never have walked again.

The fact that the event has no obvious meaning, for me, makes it more real.

It has no apparent symmetry or poetry, and I have no urge to add any. Beyond recounting it to my friend at the time, I have rarely, if ever, spoken of it, though I think of it sometimes. The writing of it has filled me with a deep, aching melancholy, coloured with a vague hope, though I don't know why or for what. I have no urge to rationalise or analyse it, or ever to go back there again.

All I can tell is what happened, what I remember, what I saw, or at least, what I think happened, if think is the right word.

Fritz
By Lisa Main

The snowcat had been bumping through a colourless void for what seemed like hours. Now as Royal Marine Captain John Hughes stared out over the barren white landscape and caught sight of the place that would be his home for the next three months, he felt as dark and despondent as the grey, snow-weighted clouds in the half light above him.

Elvergaardsmein had been a German prisoner of war camp during the Second World War and seemed to have changed very little in the forty years since it had come into allied possession. Inside the high wire fences was row after row of steel-grey Nissan huts and featureless utilitarian buildings. If ever a place had failed to have even one redeeming feature then this was it.

'Cheer up, Sir. It's not as bad as it looks from the outside.' He didn't realise his sigh had been audible until Colour Sergeant Moncrieff called out over the sound of the engine. 'Once we've got everything settled in and the main party arrives, the place comes to life and I'm told the Red House is a very comfortable billet.

'The Red House?'

'That's what they call the Officers' Mess. It'll be obvious why when you see it – completely built of brick it is. It was the Camp Commandant's house and you can bet he didn't let himself suffer any discomfort, unlike the poor buggers he was keeping here.'

'He must have been a mean bastard.' Now Sergeant Billings leaned forward and joined in the conversation. 'Even his personal staff suffered if he wasn't happy. If you see Fritz you can ask him all about that.'

Both he and Moncrieff started to laugh and John frowned.

'Who's Fritz, one of the civilian staff?'

'Not exactly, sir.' A wry smile crossed Moncrieff lips. 'Fritz has been there longer than anyone else. He's a ghost.'

John was momentarily irritated. Did they really think he was gullible enough to fall for a ploy like that? He'd been in the Corps for almost fifteen years and had heard almost every cock-and-bull story going.

'I don't believe in ghosts,' he said firmly.

Billings shook his head. 'That's what most people say at first but Fritz has a habit of changing their minds. Some of the local staff won't stay alone in any of the buildings he haunts and I can't say I blame them. Too many strange things happen round there.'

'What sort of things?' John decided to humour the pair.

'Piles of snow appearing in sealed containers, strange noises in empty buildings late at night and then of course there's the smell.'

'Smell?' This was trying to take the joke much too far. John grinned and expected his colleagues to finally crack and admit they were pulling his leg. However both men continued to look serious. Not so much as one muscle in either one's cheeks twitched.

'It's a sweet smell that lingers for ages afterwards. It's the first thing most people notice when Fritz is about.'

'It's said he was a bit limp wristed, if you know what I mean.' Moncrieff chuckled. 'The Commandant wasn't having any of that kind of thing on his camp and he had the poor lad shot. He's haunted the place ever since.'

The snowcat came to a halt and a blast of icy wind whipped into John's face as the door was opened. He already felt as though he'd entered purgatory. He didn't need ludicrous stories about a ghost to make him feel any worse.

The Red House was smaller than other messes he was used to but his cabin was comfortable and it was pleasant to find a log fire crackling in the hearth when he'd unpacked and made his way to the dining room. He was the only officer in the advance party that year and would be alone until the main detachment arrived, so his single place setting looked pitiful at the end of a table built to seat twenty. His chair scraped across the wooden floor as he pulled it out and almost at once a young woman came out of the kitchen.

'I am Sylvie, the catering manager.' Her English was perfect but she spoke with a heavy Norwegian accent. 'Would you like soup?'

'Yes, please.'

He watched her disappear back into the kitchen. She hadn't exuded any hint of warmth in their brief conversation. Come to think of it she looked like an ice maiden too, with skin that was pale to the point of translucence and hair so fair it verged on being colourless. The Aryan ideal. No wonder the Nazis had been so quick to dominate a country that had little else to offer.

She came back, put a bowl of brown liquid down in front of him and then retreated again without another word. Definitely not the friendly sort then. Perhaps it didn't pay to be. Having a figure like that and working with over a hundred men who wouldn't see their women for weeks probably exposed her to more attention than she wanted as it was.

The soup was hot and meaty with a hint of spice behind it. If all the food was going to this be this good then at least there would be one compensation for living in sub-zero temperatures and day-long darkness. John wiped the bowl clean with a slice of bread and watched in eager anticipation as Sylvie brought in the next course.

'That was delicious, thank you.'

Her reply was a tight smile. Surely it wouldn't hurt her to be a little more sociable. After all she was the only person he was likely to see until the next morning and he felt in need of some conversation before the long hours alone in his cabin, thinking of Carol and the kids. He decided to try again.

'That's a lovely perfume you're wearing.'

The thick white china plate she was holding clattered down onto the table in front of him and he thought she looked momentarily anxious before recovering herself and speaking in a voice as icy as the wind outside.

'I am not wearing any and I prefer you not to make such personal remarks.'

Hell. Now she thought he was making some kind of a pass at her.

'I'm sorry I didn't mean…'

Her mouth was set in a taut line. 'Let me make it clear immediately that I do not wish to make liaisons with anyone here. I have a fiancé in Bergen.'

She marched purposely from the room and John cursed his stupidity. Saying something like that had been stupid but passing a comment on the weather here would have been a bloody waste of time. The woman clearly didn't want to be bothered by anyone but why deny that she was wearing perfume when it was obvious that she was? Even now that she was gone, a faint trace of its floral bouquet still hung in the air.

The following morning, John wrapped himself up in his snow gear and followed the lights that led him to the main stores. Moncrieff had already organised the men into a working party and they were unpacking the containers of Arctic survival gear and skis.

'Morning, Sir.' The older man eyed him knowingly. 'You look a bit rough. Bad night was it?'

'I didn't get a lot of sleep,' John admitted. The payphone in the main corridor rang three times through the night and everyone time I went to answer the bloody thing there was no one there.'

'It could've been worse, Sir.' Billings had joined them and was grinning. 'Someone else might have picked it up and said 'Ja?'.'

Not that bloody ghost business again. John struggled to keep his temper under control. If he found out that either of this pair were behind the calls, he have them on extra duties for the next year.

'I've told you before, I don't believe in ghosts, goblins or any other kind of similar nonsense. Now I want this place organised and ready to run before the main troop arrives so let's all get on with what we're supposed to be doing.' He stomped into the small sectioned off part of the hangar that would be his office for the next three months and slammed the door so hard that the drawers in the filing cabinet rattled.

That evening he worked on after the other men had gone for supper. He wanted to be certain that every item in the store was logged in properly before Colonel Ashby arrived, and besides, he was in no hurry to encounter Sylvie again after the night before. The lamp on his desk had been on all day and when it started to flicker, he guessed that the bulb was giving out.

Housekeeping items had been unpacked in the early part of the afternoon and he had personally overseen their storage on the shelves closest to the hangar door. He had just located a box of light bulbs when there was a deafening crash in his office and he almost lost his grip on the carton. Pushing it back onto the shelf unopened, he hurried back across the hangar and closed his fingers over the door handle. It was silent inside now and all he could hear was the blood pounding in his ears as his heart slowly returned to its natural rhythm. He took a deep breath. This was ridiculous. He was letting stupid stories get to him. It was windy outside and the walls were far from adequately insulated. He'd been sitting freezing long enough to have worked that out. Something had blown over, that was all.

He entered the room and his boot crunched on broken glass. The photograph of Carol that he carried with him whenever he was away was lying in the remains of its shattered frame. He bent to pick it up and carefully eased away the last shards of glass before they could damage the picture itself. It would have to stay as it was until he got home.

'Everything all right, Sir?' The unexpected voice behind him sent his heart into his mouth and only years of training kept him from crying out when he turned to find himself only a foot away from a white hooded figure.

'Sir?' He recognised the voice and his alarm died away. He wasn't able to eradicate it entirely however and, when it spoke, it manifested itself as extreme irritation.

'Billings, what the hell are you doing back here?'

'I thought you might like some coffee as you were working so late.' The man in the Arctic suit held out a flask in his gloved hand.

'Thank you.' John took the flask and turned to put it on the desk. 'Did you bring that in with you as well?'

'What, sir?'

'You know very well what I'm talking about.' John's temper flared up. 'I don't know whose bloody idea it was to start this ghost business but I want it stopped right now. The next man who pulls an infantile prank on me will be charged with insubordination. Do you understand?'

'Sir, I don't know what -.'

'I said do you understand?' John snapped and Billings nodded, falling into a sullen silence.

'Good. Now get out and let me work in peace.'

The door banged behind the sergeant and John swept the pile of snow on his desk onto the floor.

In the days after that no one mentioned ghosts in John's presence and the jokes stopped abruptly. However, the damage had already been done. His communications with the other ranks was limited to work related matters and he was aware of their conversations stopping as soon as he entered a room. Sylvie, too, maintained her aloof silence and John felt increasingly isolated.

When the main party arrived he greeted them with relief. Sound filled the quiet corners of the camp and the Red House became a lively place that it was a pleasure to retire to each evening.

Colonel Ashby's first act upon his arrival was to hold a Mess Dinner. The wine waiters didn't allow anyone's glass to empty during the meal and by the time the port was brought to the table, John's face felt as red as the jacket of his Mess uniform. It was a long time since he'd had this much to drink. He laughed loudly at all the jokes in the speeches and wondered if it was just the alcohol or the pure exhilaration of company that was affecting him.

When the meal was over and he rose to make his way to the toilets, he discovered that his gait wasn't quite as steady as it should be. He was drunker than he'd thought.

The white tiled room was empty but it wasn't long before he came aware of another man joining him at the urinals.

'That was a good night, wasn't it?' His speech sounded slurred. He'd have a screamer of a hangover in the morning, but what the hell. It was worth it. 'Glad to have some decent company again. That Sylvie's a miserable bitch and all I could get out of the men was some crap about a ghost. As if I was going to fall for bilge like that. Have you heard the ridiculous yarns about this place?'

'I have heard some of them.'

'Oh very funny. Cut the German accent. I've had enough of the whole thing already.' John turned to good-naturedly confront his companion and then watched in horrified disbelief as the figure in front of him smiled and then faded away, leaving nothing but a sweet floral odour.

Still there…
By Hilary Halliwell

'He winks at me, you know…'

Mike looked at me half pityingly, and half
contemptuously.

'It's a bloody photograph, H, photos don't wink!
Are you still on that HRT, by the way?'

'No…' I snapped rather too quickly for my
liking.

'Thought not!' He retorted without looking up.
'Scary or what!'

The cheek of the man! What does he know about
my ghost anyway? He's far too insensitive to have a
paranormal experience, well, unless he's had ten
pints that is, and then it's more likely to be pink
elephants!

I couldn't be bothered to argue these days. My
best friend in the entire world was dead, and if I said
he winked at me, then he damn-well-did!

Mike would never understand, he was too, well,
level, I suppose. Not like me, I'm up for it you see,
the paranormal, and why not? I mean who says there
isn't an afterlife anyway? I saw my granny after she
died! There I was, sitting on the loo in her big
Victorian house in Kew Gardens, at the time of the
visitation. It was about four months after she'd

passed away, okay I was missing her dreadfully I admit, but I didn't imagine it, honestly I didn't.

We'd just moved in to Granny's house; Mum and Dad had a flat in London, so they'd no plans to move in. It was such a lovely three story Victorian house in a tree-lined avenue, full to bursting with memories of my childhood on every floor. Well, like I said, I was sat there, wasn't I, doing what you do sitting on the toilet, then, time just sort of slipped, and she was there! There, she was standing there, like it was the most natural thing in the world, and me with my knickers down round my ankles, sitting on the family seat talking to the dead!

'Hello Darling, how are you?', she said, in her soft, Scottish lilt. 'Grandpa sends his love...' she continued, just as normal as normal can be! I mean you don't make up things like that, now do you? If I were going to make up a story about a visitation from a dead loved one, well I'd at least add a bit of romance to it. White flowing robes and ghostly figures levitating in front of me at dawn, but, well I ask you, toilets, knickers round ankles, you decide, fact or fiction...

'So why hasn't Grandpa come with you?' I asked her, matter of fact.

'He's got a bit of a cold, dear, they won't let us come over if we're not well, not a hundred percent, you know.' Oh well, of course I understood now, cross infection and all that, very sensible in Heaven obviously. It gets worse doesn't it!

We'd chatted on about my first born, Matthew, and Granny had said 'Oh don't worry about baby

162

being small, dear, the little ones grow like mushrooms!'

Matt had been premature, just four pounds; it'd been a very worrying time. So that put my mind at rest, as Granny always told the truth, Granny knew everything.

Thus it'd been my first brush with the spirit world, if I were making it up I could have done a whole lot better than that!

Anyway as I told you, he winks at me, no matter what Mike says and I've even seen him out of the corner of my eye a couple of times, just off centre of my line of vision, but he's there alright and there's no mistaking him…

I think Mike's jealous, or in denial, one of the two. He was always envious of him when he was around; he always used to say things like

'You love him more than you love me, you're so affectionate to him H, so what is it about him that I don't have?'

I'd laugh and tell him not to be silly, that he was imagining it, just like when he told me that I was imagining it when he had that affair.

That's when we'd gotten so close, my best friend and me. He was already a good friend, but he was wonderful when Mike was having his fling.

There were times I thought I was going to die of a broken heart. I mean when you're heading towards forty, and the kids are becoming more independent, and you've been married since you were eighteen, you sort of think you can relax a bit and be yourself, trust who you're with. In fact for the first time in my married life I felt easy in our relationship and I did trust him. So, when out of the blue he started to change towards me, you know, coming in late, smelling of cheap perfume, turning into medallion man, well it'd devastated me and that's when my friend and I got closer every day; after all he was all I had. I'd even thought of ending it all, though I'm ashamed to admit it now.

I'd sat down by the beach on a cold March day, pondering how long it would take me to die in the freezing sea. But then I thought of my boys and my friend, and managed to walk home with some of my life and a little of my dignity still intact...

He'd saved me, so who could blame me if I had become somewhat dependent on this other male in my life?

We'd sit by the fire, and he'd listen to all my fears, he was there for me. My best friend in all the world, never judging me, just being there for me as always...

Mike and I survived the affair, and very gradually some degree of normality returned to our lives. It was interspersed with bouts of terrible insecurity on my part, but I loved Mike, so what could I do? I had to give us another chance. My friend though was very obviously anti-Mike and like the star he was he continued to support me when things were good or bad. Never asking for more than friendship or my company. Why couldn't all relationships be this good, I'd asked myself?

Fifteen years passed. My kids grew into men, Mike and I healed, and though I suffered some degree of ill health and disability life was OK, good even. Then, disaster struck…

Mike and I had been away to Rye in Sussex. We love that place. As usual I'd left my best friend to house-sitting, but when we returned a week later I knew just by looking at him that something terrible had happened, something was very wrong. He looked so old and tired, not like himself at all. Two days after our return he suffered a massive stroke; a very bright light had gone out in my world. I was inconsolable. How I drove home, that day I said a final goodbye to him, I'll never know.

Life continued and Mike was very supportive. I think, reading between the lines, he'd grown fond of him too, though I couldn't say it was ever reciprocated! I don't think he ever forgave Mike for hurting me. Sixth sense? Call it what you will.

A few months passed, and then it started. I'd sit and look at his photo that held pride of place on the bookcase opposite to where I sit in the evenings. And quite suddenly it happened. He winked at me, just like that. Just like he always used to. I rubbed my eyes in disbelief; I must be tired, I told myself. But he did it again, and again, and again. The more I returned the wink, the more he replied with those lovely eyes of his. It was such a comfort, but I knew it sounded a bit mad!

'There look, he's doing it again, look Mike, can't you see?'

Mike looks up from the racing page of the Sun. He looks over his half-moon form studying glasses at me and sighs heavily then carries on with the sports page. But I don't care, 'cos I saw him; I really did see him.

'Seriously H, get a grip old girl, go back to the doctors, there must be something else they can give you, it's the meno what's-it. Winking photos, talking to relatives on the loo, whatever next? You really do have a seriously weird imagination!'

I carried on watching Coronation Street, vowing never to say anything about it again. Perhaps I did need treatment after all. It was then, quite suddenly, that I saw him, more clearly than ever before. He was sitting there as large as life right next to Mike on the sofa. I fought to keep quiet; I couldn't take my eyes off him. He winked just like in the photo. I said his name, and patted my knee, and that's when Mike looked at me aghast.

'What now?', he said with more than a hint of exasperation in his voice.

'Look, beside you, there…' I said pointing a trembling finger.

'What are you going on about?'

But, as I looked again he'd gone and Mike looked set to call the men in white coats…

I could have reached out and touched him and now he was gone and what was worse, Mike was convinced I'd finally lost the plot.

I felt close to tears, I knew what I'd seen. I stood up to walk out into the kitchen, but just as I did so, I saw him again, that friend of mine, jumping down from the sofa, tail aloft, plodding out into the kitchen ahead of me as if to say,

'Where's my supper, Mum?'

'Look, oh-my-GOD!', said Mike, calling from the lounge. He'd turned whiter than the shirt he was wearing and was pointing to the sofa next to where he sat. There, right beside him, was the unmistakable indentation of where a very large cat had been curled up. I put my hand to the spot, it was still warm..

He still winks at me you know, my best friend in the entire world. Sometimes I talk to him, he doesn't answer but I know he's there, listening to me, taking it all in, just like he always used to. I've two rescue cats now, I know they see him too. A meow here, a hiss there, but they always show respect. No one ever sits in Rocky's place beside Mike on the sofa, or at the foot of my side of the bed. Why, just the other day, a warm sunny July day, I'm sure he followed me down the garden path, handsome chap that he is, tail up in the air, his footsteps in mine just like always…

Staying At The Grove
By Carolyn Lewis

The caravan sat neatly in the corner of the garden, whipped occasionally by the long, stately branches of an overhanging weeping willow. The roof of the caravan was carpeted by drab moss and twisted, blackened leaves from the willow. Somehow the leaves reminded me of the chocolate curls my mother always covered birthday cakes with. The caravan was empty, 'Has been for years,' Karen, the owner of the holiday house, told us. 'Mrs. Mayberry lived in there for the summer months, but she died ten years ago.' Karen was in her mid-thirties and, as she showed us around the house that was to be our home for the next fortnight, she appeared to have more enthusiasm talking about the caravan and its late occupier than she did in demonstrating the vagaries of the immersion heater and the gas cooker. 'I keep telling my husband we should get it shifted,' she told us, her smile widening as she spoke, 'but somehow, you know how it is, you never seem to get round to doing things.' My parents smiled, they nodded, they knew all about running out of time. So many things to do, that's why we'd all come on holiday, my parents, my sister Andrea and I, for a break, for relaxation.

Karen seemed in no hurry to leave us that first day, happily accepting a glass of wine from the bottle that had been left for us in the otherwise empty fridge. She'd given Andrea and me a quick smile, we were clearly too young for her to waste any of her public relations skills on. She told my parents a little bit about the house we'd rented.

'This house, The Grove, had been in the Mayberry family for years, over four hundred I believe and at one time it was a working farm; the family owned a lot of land but over the years the land was sold and now there's just the garden. When old Mrs. Mayberry died, the house came to us, well, that is my husband, he was the only relative, a nephew on his father's side.'

My sister scampered off, I knew what she'd be doing. She wanted to explore the bedrooms on her own, bag the best bed. I wanted to hear more about the caravan's tenant.

Karen told us that the last Mayberrys had been childless. 'There was a lot of gossip in the village because Ralph Mayberry was known to be a ladies' man and it was generally thought that the problem lay with her, Evelyn Mayberry. She was such a gentle creature, loved this garden and never strayed far from the house. When Ralph died,' at this point, Karen looked towards my mother, looking I felt, for female complicity in the understanding of men, 'he was in the pub, he had a heart attack as he sat at the bar and after his death, she found he'd squandered everything, left her with nothing.'

She held her glass out as my father replenished her drink, 'So what could the poor woman do? She didn't want to leave her home so she came up with the idea of renting out the house. She worked it out that if she could let it for the holiday months, May through till late September, she could afford to keep the house. That's where the caravan came in.' Karen's cheeks were a little flushed and she smiled at my parents. 'She thought that if she stayed in the caravan, out of everyone's way, then she could keep an eye on the house, check that it wasn't being wrecked, you know, kids damaging it.' She glanced in my direction as she spoke.

My mother found her voice, 'So, this woman, this Mrs. Mayberry, stayed in the caravan while strangers were living in her home? I don't think I could have done that, staying out of my house while other people lived in it.'

'Well, Evelyn Mayberry did just that - she did it for nearly ten years.'

That night I could hear my parents discussing the caravan long after my sister and I had gone to bed. Andrea had chosen the best bed, the one nearest the window, overlooking the garden and the caravan.

When we awoke the following day it was to the sight of Cornish sunshine trying to inch its way past the heavy brocade curtains in our bedroom.

'No messing about today,' Mum warned Andrea and I, 'we spent all day yesterday sitting in the car so we're heading for the beach straight after breakfast.' She stacked our cereal bowls, cups and saucers on the draining board and wiped away the crumbs of toast. 'The house is so beautiful,' she told my Dad, 'it feels such a shame to leave anything out of place.' Andrea and I barely took any notice, we

171

were far too busy collecting our fishing nets and armbands. We'd come to Cornwall for the endless stretches of sand and the thundering of the Atlantic ocean. We couldn't be bothered by whether or not plates were in the right place.

That first day was idyllic. The sun shone from a cloudless blue sky and the waves cushioned our many falls from the surfboards my Dad had hired. We ate our lunch, four Cornish pasties, on the beach and my sister and I told our parents that this was going to be the best holiday ever.

When we arrived back at our holiday home, my Dad frowned. 'I could have sworn I closed the bedroom windows.' Fanatical about security at home, he'd toured the house not long after we arrived, checking the locks and testing the catches on every window.

From inside the car, our four heads peered up and we saw the bottom of the heavy curtains rippling out from an open window. 'You must have forgotten that room, ' my mother told him as she got out of the car.

Warning us about the trouble we'd be in if we walked sand into the house, my mother opened the front door and stopped so abruptly that my sister and I cannoned into her. 'What's that smell? Can you smell it? It's as if someone's been baking cakes.'

We sniffed obediently but were unable to detect anything unusual. Smelt just like a normal house, we thought and Andrea and I made our way into the kitchen, Mum following close behind.

'Now, look at that.' she pointed dramatically to the sink and again Andrea and I failed to notice

172

anything amiss. `The sink, look at the sink,' she said firmly.

'What? What are we looking at?' I asked. 'It's just a draining board, same as the one we've got at home.'

'But where are the bowls, the cups, the things I left to drain, they've gone.'

We shrugged, Andrea and I, this was so boring, we had no interest in conversations about cups and saucers.

But Mum wouldn't let it go, 'Guess what?' she spoke to my father as he followed us into the kitchen, 'Someone's been putting things away while we've been on the beach.' My father shrugged too, `I'm more bothered by the open window. I know I closed them all before we went out.'

The mystery kept Mum and Dad intrigued for hours; all through our supper we listened to an endless discussion as to whether it was Karen who let herself in, 'Perhaps she needs to check up on us, see if we're looking after the place, or perhaps someone from the village had been employed to tidy up for us.' The talk moved from one suggestion to another until my mother finally announced, 'Well, whoever it is, I'm not sure that I like it. I'm going to ring Karen in the morning, tell her we can cope on our own.'

Late that night, I waited until I could hear Andrea's measured breathing, then I moved towards the window and perched on the end of her bed. I moved the curtains to one side so I could look at the garden. There was a full moon, its silvery metallic light glistened on the branches of the weeping willow. In the silence I thought I could hear the sound of the branches as they flicked against the dark windows of the caravan. Then I had to move, Andrea had woken up and told me to get off her bed.

The following morning Mum said before she did anything else, she was going to ring Karen, let her know that we didn't need any help, we were used to coping on our own.

When she came back into the kitchen she told my Dad that no-one had been to the house. 'Karen said it wasn't part of the rental agreement, there was no maid service.' They shook their heads as Andrea and I ate our cornflakes and toast.

That day we went to St. Ives and we had fish and chips for lunch and Andrea caught four tiny crabs, insisting that they'd be all right if she kept them in her new red bucket.

When our car stopped outside the front of the house, Mum made a joke about our 'ghosts.' Let's see what they've done today.' I noticed Dad glance up at the windows; they were all closed.

Mum went through the front door first and she began sniffing loudly. 'Lavender polish, I'd know that smell anywhere.' In the kitchen tea-towels had been draped over the taps and the wooden floor shone. My Mum put a hand to her chest, 'I don't like this very much. I definitely didn't leave the tea-towels there.'

My Dad came in, his arms wrapped around a tartan travel rug, inflatable water rings, two fishing nets and a silver Thermos flask. 'Coming home to a clean house isn't too bad though, is it?'

Mum looked at him, 'Well no, but I'm not sure that I like someone else clearing up after me - especially when I don't know who it is, or how they get in'

Dad winked at Andrea and me and said he thought he'd check out the local pub later on that evening.

After he'd gone we washed up the plates and cutlery from our supper and Mum said she'd like to have a look at the garden. I knew what she really wanted was to look at the caravan. Andrea decided to watch television so once everything had been cleared away, Mum carefully draping the tea-towels over the taps, we opened the back door.

'Oh, this is lovely,' she said. 'Look at the roses, I've never seen so many different varieties.' She named a few, didn't mean anything to me, but I could smell their perfume. Mum touched a leaf, 'Look, no black spot or greenfly, these leaves are beautifully clean and glossy. Someone must spend a lot of time here, tending these roses.'

It was a big garden and Mum took ages looking at all the flowers and plants but finally, we reached the caravan. In the daylight it looked awful. Black mould had formed on the windows and there was muddy coloured moss growing around the top of the door. There were small steps close to the front door and Mum stood on them and tried the door handle. It rattled but the door didn't move.

Suddenly I felt very cold and I saw Mum wrap her arms around her chest. 'Who on earth would want to live here, in this?' She stepped down and peered into the windows. The glass was filthy and she rubbed at it with her hand. 'Can't see a thing in there. I wonder why no-one has moved this; it spoils the look of the garden.'

I was really cold and told Mum I wanted to go back to the house. She nodded and we moved away. Then I heard a thump as if something or someone had fallen over. 'What was that?' We both looked towards the caravan. Was it moving? It seemed to be rocking. I blinked and looked again. Nothing. It looked just the same.

I got out of bed again that night and peered out between the curtains. No moon glistened on the weeping willow. The caravan looked very dark. Just then I heard the back door close. The door was heavy and Dad said it had been warped by rain. When it was closed it scraped across the floor, I heard the scraping noise.

I looked over towards Andrea's bed. She was lying on her back, one leg kicked out over the eiderdown. The bucket with the crabs was next to her bedside cabinet. I left her there and went downstairs.

It was only when I reached the bottom of the stairs that I felt frightened. I thought that if someone was there, they'd certainly hear me, they'd hear the thumping of my heart.

There was no carpet on the hallway, just black and white marble tiles and I could feel my bare feet getting colder as I stood there staring towards the kitchen. There was no sound from behind the door and all I could hear were the springs of a bed as upstairs someone turned over.

I told myself that we were the only ones in the house, and I moved towards the kitchen door, my hand outstretched to push it open. It moved silently and I stared in. The kitchen was empty and the only sound was the drip of a tap. There was a funny smell, it wasn't unpleasant, just a warm earth sort of smell. I closed the door behind me and went back to bed.

The following day I told no-one about the noise I'd heard and, by the time I'd come down for breakfast, the funny smell had gone; it had been replaced by the comforting aroma of toast.

My mother was being very cheerful and told Andrea and I that we were going back to the beach. 'We came for a holiday and that's what we're going to have.' She made sandwiches and packed up our picnic basket. Before we left the kitchen that day, she neatly folded the tea-towels over the backs of the kitchen chairs.

Mum made a few jokes about our 'ghost' and I noticed she kept looking at her watch as we built sandcastles and ate our sand-encrusted ham sandwiches. Dad told her he hadn't paid any extra for the ghostly housework and she should think herself lucky. They pretended to Andrea and me that they weren't bothered by the whole thing.

But then, not long after lunch, Mum said she wanted to go back to the house. 'It looks as if it might rain,' she told us. There wasn't a cloud in the sky.

They argued, Mum and Dad while Andrea and I packed up our wet swimming costumes and tried to get the sand out of our shoes. Before long we'd stopped the car outside the front door of The Grove. My Dad was muttering about 'damn fool nonsense,' as he grabbed hold of our wet towels. Mum stood silently near the front door. 'You go in first' she told him. Without a word, just a baleful glance at her, he put the key in the lock. The door swung open and the four of us stood on the porch.

'Oh, for God's sake,' my Dad was annoyed and he pushed past us to go into the hallway. Andrea, Mum and I watched as he walked to the foot of the stairs. 'What are you waiting for?' he asked, 'the house is as we left it, look.' Only then did Mum venture in, holding our hands.

'That smell, what on earth is that awful smell?' she glanced around, 'it's coming from upstairs.' She gazed at my father with worry in her eyes. 'Go and see what it is, please.'

With a dramatic sigh he ran up the stairs. We heard him open the door to their bedroom, then there was silence.

'John?' My Mum called, her voice hoarse, 'Is everything all right?'

There was no sound.

'John?'

Then he appeared, looking down at us from the landing. The colour had drained from his face and the sunburnt patches on his forehead looked at odds with the pallor of his skin.

'Don't come up, leave it to me,' his voice was rough, abrupt and he disappeared back into the bedroom. My Mum put her hands on Andrea's shoulders and she propelled her into the kitchen. I was left at the foot of the stairs, listening to a series of thumps coming from the back bedroom.

From the kitchen my mother called me, 'Carolyn, come in here please, now.'

I thought if I didn't answer she'd think I hadn't heard her and I ran up the stairs. The thumping noises were louder and I could hear the sound of Dad's breathing through the closed door. I tried the handle and pushed the door open.

'Like a bomb has hit it,' that's what my mother used to say about the state of my bedroom, but this room looked as if two bombs had exploded in it. All the clothes in the wardrobes were lying on the floor, the purple eiderdown had been thrown against the dressing table and the rest of the bedding lay in a heap near the foot of the bed. Both bedside cabinets had been overturned and Dad was trying hard to put them back on either side of the bed. The smell up here was awful, pungent and eye-watering. My dad grunted when he saw me, 'Where's your mother?'

'She's downstairs, with Andrea. Dad, what happened? Where is that smell coming from?'

'Never mind all that, just give me a hand with this - God knows what your mother will do if she sees this.'

I held my breath and picked up clothes and coat hangers and began to shove everything back into the wardrobe. Each time I had to breathe, I held my hand over my mouth. Dad didn't say another word until he'd remade the bed and opened the window as wide as it would go. Almost immediately the smell left the room and I breathed normally again.

179

Dad's mouth was set in a hard line and he told me to go downstairs, into the kitchen, 'Make sure your mother's all right. I'm going to make some phone calls. Not here, I'll ring from the phone box down the road.'

He urged me downstairs, nudging me with his hand, 'Don't tell your mother, not one word.'

'But what'll I say?'

'No idea, just don't tell her about what you saw.'

When I went into the kitchen, Mum was sitting at the table, a crumpled handkerchief balled up in her fist. Andrea was drinking milk and she had a frothy moustache around her top lip.

'Where's your Dad?' Mum's eyes were darting around, looking over my head, towards the door, 'Is he still upstairs?'

'No,' I mumbled, 'he's gone outside for a bit, he won't be long.'

I didn't know what to say if Mum asked anything about what had been going on upstairs but oddly enough she didn't say a word, just asked if I wanted a drink of milk. When I said that I did, she also brought out a packet of ginger biscuits and Andrea and I sat at the table in almost total silence.

I looked around the kitchen and it looked the same to me, that is the same as when we'd left it that morning. Mum was drumming her fingers on the table and she jumped when we heard Dad coming into the house.

'John?' She stood up, 'Where have you been?'

Dad glanced at me, 'To make a phone call. I've been trying to get to the bottom of this, and I thought I should talk to Karen.'

'What happened upstairs?' Mum had moved closer to Dad and he put his hand out to touch her arm. 'Nothing much,' again he glanced at me. 'Just a bit of a mess up there, that's all.'

Mum's eyes were locked on his. 'A bit of a mess,' she repeated. 'What did Karen say? Does she know why these things are happening…did you tell her about the smell?'

Dad nodded, 'I told her everything and she hasn't got a clue. She says that no-one has ever had any trouble before. People come back here year after year. She wonders if we left a window or a door open, perhaps someone got in, some kids wanting to make a nuisance of themselves.'

'Kids? How can anyone get in? We lock everything up and even if it was kids, that doesn't explain the smell.'

Dad gave a brief smile, 'Well actually Karen said we should remember that this used to be a farm and there are still farms nearby. She asked if we'd ever heard of muck-spreading. Felt a bit of a berk when she said that to be honest. Never gave it a thought.'

He was so anxious to bring events back to normal and he smiled at us, 'Makes sense when you think about it.'

Mum sat back and sighed. 'I'm not sure, perhaps we should leave.'

'Mum!' Both Andrea and I wailed and Dad shook his head.

'No, we won't do that. We've let the situation get on top of us. We need to keep a rational head, that's all.'

Mum allowed herself to be persuaded and we had a tea-party and planned what we'd do the next day. We opened the back door and the smell of the roses crept into the kitchen and my parents discussed whether they should grow roses at home.

I left them there amidst the tea-cups and biscuit wrappers and walked out into the garden. I wanted to see the caravan again, I'm not sure why unless it was to see if it had changed in some way since we'd arrived.

It sat squat and ugly looking exactly the same; the mark where Mum had rubbed the window clearly visible. I stood on the top step and shook the door handle.

All I could hear was the rattle of the branches of the weeping willow. I stepped back onto the path. As I looked up, one of the grubby net curtains moved. It shook as if someone was holding it, peering out from inside the caravan. My mouth was very dry and I could form no words. I stared hard but saw nothing. I must have watched that window for ten minutes, but there were no further movements.

I turned to go back to the house but couldn't resist one last look at the caravan. I had the unnerving sensation that I was being watched, that someone was staring at me. Once more I looked towards the window and this time I saw a woman's face: a lined, old face with unkempt grey hair. Some instinct made me put a hand up as if to wave and the movement was enough to frighten the woman, her face blurred, became invisible.

I ran to the house, almost falling into the kitchen. It looked so normal, biscuit crumbs scattered on the table, mugs of tea and glasses of milk adding to the general clutter. It was the normality that decided it for me, I told no-one that I'd seen a face, an old lady's face.

The next day we visited St. Ives again, enjoying the sunshine, splashing in the robust waves, catching crabs to replace the ones that had died.

This time when we returned to the house, it was Mum who unlocked the door; moving slowly towards the kitchen, her head held high before turning, with a beam on her face to tell us, `Nothing, I can't smell a thing.'

There were no more smells, no more displaced tea-towels, no more disturbances of any kind for the rest of our stay.

Good Neighbours
By Jan Jones

Up until now, my only supernatural experiences have been with departed cats. I have had a fair number of these - the sense of fur rubbing fleetingly against my ankles, the weight of a sleeping body on my feet at night, the faint echo of a homecoming call on the air at dawn - but never anything more..

I'm not sure even now whether this story counts as scary, exactly, but as it has certainly spooked me, I'll leave you to be the judge.

Two nights ago I had a dream. Nothing unusual in that. In my dream I was in my back garden and Katie Fforde the novelist was advising me of all the things I would need to do before moving to the north of England. I'm not moving to the north of England, by the way, and why Katie Fforde, who lives in Gloucester, should have been telling me about it remains a mystery. Possibly the fact that I'd just finished re-reading her novel Highland Fling had something to do with it. Anyway, there we were in my back garden and Jean-next-door was in her back garden too, bustling about with a tape measure.

Now, because it was a dream, I didn't feel at all surprised that Jean was there when in fact she died five years ago. I was just really glad to see her outside enjoying the sunshine. I was even more pleased to see that Tony, her husband, was also outside, quietly getting on with some carpentry. 'Oh good,' I thought, 'he's found her again. Now they'll be back to normal and everything will be all right for him at last.' Because I'd been to Tony's funeral just the previous week, you see, and in any case the house next door hasn't felt right since he first went into hospital.

At this point I ought to tell you about Jean and Tony. We'd been neighbours for over twenty years, and I think I can honestly say I've never known a closer couple. Not in a lovey-dovey way, more kind of settled, here we are and here we stay, sort of thing. Partly, I suppose, it was because they'd never had children and there weren't even any relatives any more, so they depended on each other for companionship. Oh, there were times when they had a good old shouting match up and down the length of the garden, but what couple doesn't row now and again? It never seemed to make a difference to their relationship.

The other thing which I was particularly pleased to see in my dream was that Tony was building something against the back of the house. Some sort of wooden rack, it looked like. He loved woodwork, loved making useful, practical things. He thoroughly enjoyed crafting cupboards for instance, to fit into awkward, fiddly places and you should just see the beautifully ordered racks and shelves in his garage. It nearly broke my heart to see the way the valuers swept all his jars of carefully graduated screws and nails into the skip the day they cleared the place ready to sell. Anyway, Tony hadn't done any woodwork at all since Jean had died, hadn't so much as picked up a chisel. His workshop at the top of the garden had stayed silent and empty, gathering dust and all his tools with it.

The heart went out of him the day she died, that's how it struck me. He still walked the dog, but the walks were shorter. His conversations over the back gate rambled. He didn't play the piano any more. His television went on earlier in the mornings and stayed on later at night. He turned the sound up louder. As time went on he stopped eating properly, sometimes didn't bother shaving or putting on a shirt. The day he collapsed and was taken into hospital, he didn't want to come out.

But hospitals can't afford bed-blockers, so they sent him home after three weeks with a diet sheet. His friends visited even more regularly and found him a home help. The people over the road took the dog for walks. I got his coal in, put out his rubbish and ran him up to the shop for cigars and ready meals. Everyone got used to his fretful phone calls.

Despite the care, his health deteriorated. A district nurse was organised. We added taking in drinks and doing his shopping to the things we did for him. The phone calls increased. He grew forgetful, distressed, confused, peevish. Horrible to watch. He went into hospital again, this time after falling and fracturing his hip, and this time he didn't come out. The past few months shuttling between ward and nursing home were the last straw for him, loss of dignity as well as loss of his reason for living. Even as I cried through his funeral, I rejoiced that he didn't have to go dragging himself on any more.

So anyway, that explains why I was so pleased to see them both in the garden in my dream. Jean, as I said, was bustling about with a tape measure in quite her old way, busy and talking nineteen to the dozen as she did so. 'Now, this bit will be yours,' she said briskly. She smiled at me as if she had a great deal to do and indicated a strip of her back garden. 'You will take care of it, won't you?'

'Yes, of course,' I replied, not knowing what on earth she was talking about. Beyond her, Tony smiled and nodded and continued to fit pieces of wood together in the sunshine. I smiled especially warmly at him, so glad that he was content again.

And that's all, really. That's the whole dream. But not quite the whole story.

Because the post has just arrived. On top of the pile is a letter from the executor of Tony's will.

Now I know what Jean was doing with that tape measure. Now I understand what she was talking about and why Tony was smiling and nodding.

All I did was take his rubbish out and get him in a bit of shopping. The sort of thing any neighbour would do for anybody.

He's left us all a share in his estate.

Friends Forever
By Jill Stitson

When my best friend Alison lay dying, her icy hand in my warm one, I experienced a moment of sheer terror and a violent urge to tear myself away as I felt her spirit desperately trying to invade mine.

The first signs of the nightmare I was about to enter had all started three months earlier as Alison and I sat together in our art evening class.

'I don't feel well, Jan,' she had said turning to me, her face white.

'Oh you poor love.' I looked away from my lopsided attempt at an orchid and gazed at Ali's pale face.

Normally she had vivid colouring; rich auburn hair, unusual green-hazel eyes and a creamy skin.

'Come on, let's go,' I said, scooping up her perfect painting of the exotic purple orchid and briefly thinking how like Ali it was – beautiful and vibrant.

We left the building to the concerned mutterings of Greg, our dishy art teacher and I drove Ali home. Her husband Richard made worried noises much the same as Greg had done – men always fussed over Ali – and I promised to ring the next day.

After I had dropped her off, I pondered over my friendship with Alison. We had met at college twenty years earlier. I was round, mousy and ordinary and Ali was a sylph-like, striking redhead but we had clicked immediately. She was attractive and friendly with a great sense of humour and was just as nice to the girls as to the guys and I always wondered why she had chosen me as her friend.

'Why do you say she chose you?', my husband Bob would ask irritably. 'You don't *choose* friends in that way, it just happens.' But I knew differently.

We had a great time together, Ali and I. We would go dancing and she would light up a room as soon as she walked in, a brilliantly coloured shawl carelessly flung over her shoulders or green ribbons in her wonderful hair. She could have had any man she wanted but she would only laugh and shrug them off and eventually married Richard who was twenty years older than she was and didn't mind that she couldn't have children.

'No such thing as destiny or grand passions for me,' she would smile.

'You are my true friend Jan, forever. Your children will be my children.' I was too busy bringing up Katie and Ben to question this slightly weird statement. It was only later that I had really thought about it.

I rang Ali the next day and she said she was fine, so we arranged to meet at 'Rendezvous', a little French bistro where Ali was always given the best seat.

'Over here Jan,' she called from her favourite place by the window.

190

'Oh you look much better,' I bent to kiss her cheek which felt cold under the carefully applied makeup.

We chatted easily as always and I puzzled again as to why Ali had so few friends, especially as she had no family. Her adoptive parents were dead and she lacked any curiosity regarding her natural mother. As we got up to leave, she stumbled slightly and immediately Pierre, the head waiter, had his hand under her elbow.

'I'm fine, really, I just caught my heel,' she gave him a dazzling smile and I grinned wryly to myself – yet another scalp for Ali's belt!

A few days later Ali range me late in the evening.

'I'm scared Jan,' she said, ' I keep getting these dizzy spells and I just *know* something's really wrong and Richard's away.'

'OK,' I said soothingly. 'You go to bed and I'll ring you first thing tomorrow and we'll sort it out.'

I went with Ali to the GP the following day and he arranged for a blood test. She was eventually diagnosed with anaemia and was prescribed pills, but she didn't seem to get any better. Her dependence on me was now very obvious and Bob started to resent the time I spent with her, but she was my best friend. What could I do?

One day I determined to have some time to myself and, unlike me, went on a rare shopping spree. It felt marvellous. I found myself trying on clothes I wouldn't have looked at twice – far too exotic for me, much more Ali's style – and bought a beautiful pashmina in electric blue plus an expensive bottle of perfume.

I arrived home to an empty house and went upstairs. Rummaging in my make-up bag, I gave myself the 'full works' – eyeshadow and black eyeliner, blusher and vivid red lipstick and lashings of the perfume I had bought. On hearing the family return, I threw on the pashmina and descended the stairs.

'What do you think?' I said, dramatically spreading my arms. There was a moment of complete silence and then:

'Mum, you look awful, you're trying to copy Ali and it doesn't work.' Katie looked disgusted as only a fourteen year old can, and flung up the stairs.

Bob said, 'My God, you're even wearing her perfume.' And finally six year old Ben burst into tears and screamed 'I want my mummy!'

The spell that had surrounded me all afternoon broke, and I locked myself in the bathroom scrubbing away at the smell and aura of Ali.

Later that evening, when order had been restored, the children were in bed and I was safe in the curve of Bob's arms, I turned to him.

'I don't know what happened to me this afternoon,' I whispered. 'I don't know why I bought the perfume or the pashmina. I'm scared Bob.'

Bob made soothing noises and said I was overtired, I'd been worrying too much about Ali. I was only too happy to believe him.

The weeks passed and Ali's health weakened, I had the strange feeling that her strengths and personality were becoming mine. I inadvertently found myself saying the things she would say and doing the things she would do; even at the art class I could not escape. My paintings became Ali's paintings – clever, full of life and colour. It was as if her hand guided mine and Greg would look at me with the admiration that had once been reserved for her. On the few occasions we went to 'Rendezvous', Pierre hovered over me as he had once hovered over Ali. I enjoyed none of these attentions.

'This is ridiculous Alison,' I said one day, knowing she would understand what I meant. 'What's happening, what are you doing to me?' But then I felt stupid and cruel. Of course nothing was happening. Poor Ali was ill and I was imagining everything, wasn't I?

'Don't worry Jan, everything is as it should be.' She gazed at me with calm hypnotic eyes and I felt powerless. I tried to share my feelings with Bob but he was having a particularly difficult time at work and barely even noticed what he was eating before he fell into bed at night. The children sensed something was wrong but seemed reluctant to say anything after the fiasco of the new pashmina.

Things came to a head when Ali was rushed to hospital with pneumonia. She was dying and as I held her hand I *knew* she was trying to live through me. I was her only and final bold bid for immortality.

Suddenly I was thrust aside as doctors and nurses hurried to her bed. I caught snippets of conversation. 'Very unusual form of leukaemia. Should have been diagnosed before. At least we know how to treat her now.'

Three days later I sat by Ali's beside. The old bloom had returned to her cheeks. She was still weak but I knew that I was safe now – back to being just me.

'You're an angel Jan, what would I do without you? I'll never die while I have you,' she smiled.

The answering smile froze my lips as I realised what this really meant.

Wish Man's Wood
By Raymond Humphreys

'Three, three, the Ri-i-i-vals!
Two, two, the lily white boys,
Dressed up all in green-o-o-'
Or was it two for the rivals? He still wasn't sure, and anyway it was too late for that now.

Tony picked his way carefully up the stony path that led away from the beach. It wasn't long before the only sign of his friends was the faint glow made in the night sky by the barbecue fire. Even the sound of their campfire singing was muffled by the roar of the breaking waves. He felt very much alone.

'One is one and all alone and ever more shall be so'. He could remember that line well enough. It didn't seem a very fair way of picking someone to leave the barbecue early so as to light the fire back in the camp. His troop leader, Dennis, has suggested someone should get the billycan boiling. Tony thought that was a good idea, and had said so enthusiastically. Until that 'someone' had turned out to be Tony, that was. Why couldn't the scoutmaster have found some other way to choose someone? Just because he couldn't remember the words to a stupid song!

And now there was nothing much else in his head but Victor's story. The thought of that story grew stronger as he climbed up the path. It had all seemed like great fun the day before, when he and some of the other boys had been gathered around old Victor and his tractor. The sun had been shining then, and the boys were still hot with the thrill of having been allowed to drive the tractor. It had been Tony himself who had changed the mood by asking the question:

'What's all that you were telling the scoutmaster about then, Victor? Something about the farm being haunted?'

'Oh, 'tis nothing. Just an old story they like to tell in these parts. I promised that I wouldn't repeat it to you boys.'

'Come on Victor. Don't be a spoilsport. We won't tell anyone you've said anything. Tell us the story. We're not little kids, you know.'

Victor's dark eyes had glittered and his voice became low and confidential in tone as he spoke. The circle of boys had drawn in more tightly, as if to keep the secret from escaping.

'Well ... if you promises not to say anything.' He looked around at his fellow-conspirators, as if assessing their reliability before going on. 'There's some that say there were a monastery here in Berrynarbor, hundreds of years ago now. It were built right there in the middle of that there field where you'm boys got your tents.' Here he nodded his head and fixed his eyes in the direction of the scouts' camp site. Some of the boys, including Tony, found themselves turning their heads involuntarily to look behind them.

'It weren't such a big monastery,' continued Victor. 'But it were said to be important here in North Devon. When they weren't a-praying and a-singing hymns, the monks used to grow apples for to make cider. That cider were so good that they had to send twelve barrels of it every year to the King in London.

'It were the cider that were the cause of all the trouble, really. The local Lord, or Baron or whatever he were, he said that the apple-orchard were rightly on his land, and so he were always on to the Abbot to give him half of the cider. But the Abbot wouldn't do that and said that the Baron was a wicked, shameful man.

'And it do seem like that were true, because one day when the Abbot was off on a visit or some pilgrimage to Canterbury - they used to do that back then y'know - the Baron found some way of poisoning the apples while they were still on the trees. They say it were done by some spell or enchantment.

'Anyways, soon after that the Abbot rode back to the monastery grounds after his journey to Canterbury. A couple of the monks had gone with him, and they were singin' and a prayin' that they'd all come back in time for the harvest. For the first windfall apples were just on the ground and 'twere the custom for the Abbot to taste one of them himself before the cider-making could start. Well, even afore he went back into the monastery - he

197

were a strivin' man, see - he stopped and picked up an apple and took a bite out of it.

'Everything seemed all right at first. The Abbot smiled and nodded like, to show it were another good harvest. But then a look came over his face - a horrible look they say it were - and he fell over, twitching, like the very Devil had come into him through the apple. It weren't long before he died. But before he did, he had a vision showing him that the Baron were to blame for all this. His very last words were to order the monks to cut down the apple-trees, and to plant a copse of oak where the orchard had stood.

'Well, that they did, but the odd thing was the oak-trees never grew proper. They were always twisted and stunted. They called the copse Wish Man's Wood. Why, I don't know, but they say that the Baron fell ill when they started cutting down the apple trees and that he upped and died at the very moment that the first acorn were planted.

'The monastery was pulled down fifty or so years after that, but Wish Man's Wood is still there today. And the Abbot still walks in it, folks believe. They say that sometimes he comes down, apple in his hand, to look for his monastery. The grey monk they do call him.'

'Oh, come off it Victor! You're making it all up!' This was Dennis, the oldest of the boys present, and something of a live wire. 'I bet nobody's ever seen him. I bet you haven't, have you?'

'No, I've not seen him. They do say that anybody who sees him goes mad. His face is terrible to look at. He's not like your Friar Tuck you know, all fat and jolly. The poison in that apple made him die a horrible death, and his face is gaunt and grey. And they say that he won't rest until he passes that apple on to someone. Like passing on a curse, sort of thing.'

'Well.' Tony felt a need to show a bravado beyond that given by the warmth of the summer's day, and to support Dennis's doubting words. 'I'd never be frightened by that story.'

But now, alone on the cliff-top path there was no sunlight or circle of friends to reassure him, and his youthful cynicism was no match for the fears brought on by the darkness. He was grateful indeed for the flashlight that the scoutmaster had given him, though he wished it didn't light up the gnarled and twisted trees in quite the way it did. Could this be the edge of Wish Man's Wood? Certainly the trees were stunted and ill-formed. Thank goodness the path only seemed to skirt around the edge of the copse. The blackness of the interior seemed solid and forbidding. It was even impenetrable to the powerful beam of his flashlight.

A gentle breeze came up, bringing a chill to the air of the summer night. The branches of the trees danced and swayed in a way that Tony would not have expected them to do in such a light wind. Their leaves shimmered and rustled noisily. Tony imagined their voices whispering in his ear, voices that were taunting him with words that were somehow beyond the edge of his understanding.

Then he thought that he heard his own name being called in a deeper, clearer note that sounded from within the shadows that marked the depths of the wood. And then... silence. The sudden and absolute quiet was even more disturbing than had been the eerie call of the trees, but somehow Tony summoned the last shreds of his courage and kept on walking.

He could feel a choking dryness in his throat by the time he at last put the copse behind him, and was grateful to see the campsite not far below where he now stood. The moon was full and bright in the sky as it emerged from behind a dark cloud and here, away from the shadows of the trees, it lit up the path well. He hurried on, feeling greater relief with each step that took him away from the tortured shapes of what he was now convinced was Wish Man's Wood.

Down at the campsite the wood was dry, there was plenty of tinder so it wasn't long before Tony succeeded in getting a good fire going. As the flames rose higher the burning logs gave off a reassuring crackle, and the familiar smell of smoking wood soon filled his grateful nostrils. It was really quite pleasant to sit here alone and watch the small sparks spiralling skyward. His fears of just a short time ago were already starting to seem foolish. All the same, he was glad in the knowledge that his friends would soon return. He was even more pleased that there were good supplies of wood and water at hand, so he didn't need to think of leaving the security of the fireside to boil the billycan.

He was even considering toasting some bread over the flames. The others would appreciate that when they returned from the beach, even though they'd just come from a barbecue. But suddenly the moon passed behind some more cloud, and as it did so Tony became aware of a presence behind him, in the direction of the copse. All the details of Victor's story, now made the more terrible by the thought of the unnatural place that lay behind him, were rekindled in his mind. He dared not look around. Instead he bolted into the tent and zipped down the door. Then he waited, hardly daring to breathe.

The night was as silent as only a night in the country can be, and his ears were straining to hear anything at all. At last, after what seemed an age, Tony could hear the soft tread of footsteps outside. They were slowly, very slowly, coming in his direction. Then, with a terrified fascination, he watched as a figure slowly became darkly outlined on the firelit wall of the tent. It was that of a man, tall and thin. The lower part of the figure was not sharply visible, but the head was unmistakably cowled. For a long time it seemed to be looking down at the fire, but then it turned towards the tent.

It was too much for Tony. He buried his head as deeply as he could in his arms, flung himself onto his sleeping-bag, and waited for he knew not what.

'Oi! Wake up, Tony.' A hand was roughly shaking Tony's shoulder. He sat up, blinking slowly into the face of Dennis. 'You're a fine one. You were supposed to boil the water for the tea.'

Some moments passed before Tony could answer. 'S-sorry. I fell asleep. I had an awful dream.' He noticed for the first time that Dennis appeared tired and drawn, as if he was coming down with flu or something. Despite the way he felt himself, he wanted to say something that would cheer up his troop-leader. 'But I did put the billycan on to boil.'

'Yes, and you've nearly let it boil dry as well.' There was no doubt about it. Dennis did look strained. Not like his usual cheery self at all. 'Oh, here,' said Dennis, fumbling in his pocket for something. 'You have been careless tonight. You must have dropped this by the fire.'

Tony stared in disbelief at Dennis's outstretched hand. It held a round, succulent-looking red apple.

Screams From Purgatory
By Patricia Scott

As a young Army wife I found our last posting in Liebenau, Germany, isolated in the extreme. It was a forty minute drive in an Army ambulance to the nearest Army hospital in Hanover. But it was some improvement on our first quarters, a ground floor flat in what had been the Gestapo headquarters in Warendorf. Steel blinds over windows and doors like a fortress, and a long drive from the Army R.C.T. camp in Munster.

Our first look at Liebenau was not reassuring. Its large iron gates gave away immediately what it had once been, a Russian prisoner of war camp and only a small step up from a concentration camp. We christened it Butlins Holiday Camp. Its grim history spoke for itself when we saw our married quarters, which were primitive and basic. They had once housed the German guards.

The camp was surrounded by thick, dark pine woods. There were no wild flowers such as primroses or bluebells, and herds of tusked wild boar and shy deer roamed in them. Red squirrels were brave enough to come for the food left on our windowsills, despite the noisy army vehicles constantly moving around in the camp.

There was only one Army bus a week to the nearest NAAFI shop and an Army library in Verdon. We had to make do with this or shop in the local German village where Oxo cubes, Cornflakes and joints of lamb were unknown. As the Regimental Quartermaster, my husband Ron came to the rescue, and gave up part of his weapons store to enable us to have a small NAAFI shop in the camp. For entertainment we rigged up a makeshift cinema. Best of all we could use the large square reservoir of water, which was officially for use in case of a fire, as a swimming pool. Fire was a hazard to be avoided at all costs. The camp was built close to an ammunition dump where the Russians had worked, some committed suicide by swallowing gunpowder, preferring death to the life to which they were daily subjected.

We hadn't been there long before we picked up stories of screams heard in the Army barracks, which was unnerving for the lads and for us. But at that time everything was unsettling. The Russians were making things difficult for us with the 'Cold War', and the men were called out on 'Quick Train' manoeuvres at two and three in the morning. Families were warned to keep cases packed ready for wives and children to take flights back to England as we were based right on the Russian sector. The Army nurses would have to see to the wounded men not expectant mums. I didn't relish this as I was pregnant.

We had our lighter moments though, with our Wives club and coffee mornings. But we were given a scare one morning when some ghostly raps on my outside wall interrupted our lively meeting and we took a look outside. There was no one there.

This happened on three mornings till we nervously joined hands and said, 'Is there anyone there?' We didn't get an answer.

However, a week later we discovered the culprit. It was a large green woodpecker who had taken to tapping the wooden house beams for insects. All this was laughable and after that we made the most of the entertainment in the camp with balls, parties and regimental dinners during the winter months when we had our men in the camp.

However, one cold night we were forced to stop laughing at those who said the camp was haunted. My friend Shirley Curtis, whose quarter was two doors along from ours, was in the habit of leaving her small son Jimmy in the care of Trevor, a young serviceman, who acted as babysitter. Most of the lads enjoyed doing this. They could watch TV and if they were taking a course, could study in peace.

We had just got home from a regimental dinner when Ken, Shirley`s husband, knocked on our door. Said they had found Trevor in a state of shock and they couldn't get much sense out of him. Trevor, pale faced and shaking, greeted my husband with a garbled explanation.

'I had a beer and fell asleep watching TV. Then I heard something going on upstairs, footsteps shuffling overhead and loud cries. Scared me stiff it did, but I had to go up and see what was wrong, Q. The screams and moans coming from Jimmy`s room were that terrible. I thought he was in pain, hurt or something. Thought he'd fallen out of the cot perhaps.'

Ron lit a cigarette for the boy. 'And?'

Trevor focussed his eyes on the wall behind us; he was obviously still hearing what had frightened him so much. 'I threw the door wide open but I could see nothing, nothing at all.' He looked at us now, shaking his head, looking bewildered. 'Jimmy was still asleep in his cot but it was so cold in there, freezing, ' he said, and gripped the arm of the easy chair with a white knuckled hand. 'And I felt so bad about those screams. It was like someone was being tortured. Like they were coming from Hell. I had to bring Jimmy down, Q. Couldn't leave him up there not after that. Couldn't leave him down here on his own neither...'

It was obvious to all of us that Trevor was suffering from acute shock. Nauseated by his experience he'd brought up his supper, and his teeth chattered like castanets on the whisky glass. Ron saw to it that he went into the Medical Centre close by and was given a sleeping draught and put to bed. It didn't bear thinking what had happened in that Guards' quarters. After that Jimmy always came into our house with my children when we all had an evening out in the mess.

I thought afterwards that Trevor was more than likely able to tune into such things and was perhaps a natural medium. He'd been one of those that had heard screams in the barracks and he quickly got a posting quickly to another company. Afterwards prayers were said in the Army Chapel and the first winter snow fell and transformed everything in the camp with its glistening white blanket while the happy children made snowmen in the gardens. A troupe of fifteen young Fijians were posted to 66 Company, far away from their island in the sun, and they sang Christmas carols beautifully for us in Polynesian and French as they strolled around the married quarters on Christmas Eve.

I remember Liebenau as clearly as when I first saw it, and often wonder if, with the military gone from the place, those poor tormented souls haunt it still... but this I shall never know.

The House Next Door
By Dawn Wingfield

To a girl raised in a neat little pre-war semi, 1589 East Willow Street, Cedar Bend, Iowa, was a dream come true.

'Oh, Mac…' I sighed, as we stepped over the threshold, into an entry hall with a gleaming oak floor and a gracious, curving staircase. I couldn't stop darting around, examining the original woodwork and all the enchanting, old-fashioned details; unexpected little flights of steps leading into rooms with picture rails, bumpy walls and stained glass windows. I knew I could happily spend the rest of my life within these walls.

In the two years since Mac had whisked me away from my bank job in north London, we'd lived in a series of little condos and apartments. Now my husband's prospects had improved a bit, we were house hunting. So far, we'd looked at three homes, lacklustre tract homes with dreary basements and dark wood kitchens. 1589 East Willow Street was the fourth house on our list, and I was in love.

'I wonder if they've made a mistake with the price,' I fretted, looking down at the information our estate agent had provided us with. 'It seems very reasonable.'

'Not everyone wants to live in a place that's over a hundred years old,' Mac pointed out.

We stepped outside, into a sunny back garden with a tangly hedge of pink roses just coming into bloom, and several mature fruit trees. I thought I'd faint with joy.

'Hmm...' Mac murmured, looking around critically. 'It needs a lot of work, inside and out.'

'It seems to have a lot of space though,' I said. 'And I don't mind spending some time fixing it up.'

He sighed. 'You're crazy about it, aren't you?'

I nodded, and hurled myself into his arms. 'God, I love it, Mac! Did you see the windows, the way the light shines through the stained glass and colours everything like a jewel? And the main bedroom was perfect! I'll die if we can't make an offer.'

'We'd better make an offer then,' he said, and kissed me slowly and thoroughly, in a way that almost made me forget all about the house. Then he added, 'But first we'll get someone independent to check it out.'

As we turned to go back inside I glanced up at the house next door, shielding my eyes from the sun and squinting up. It was beautiful, a sprawling, whimsical turn of the century extravagance, with pale green paint coming away in curls and a turret rising majestically from one corner. Imagine living in a house with a turret, I thought, smiling. And then in spite of the bold May sunshine, I shivered.

Three weeks later I was sitting in the middle of an ocean of boxes, happily trying to unpack. Everything had happened so quickly after we'd started negotiating and signed papers. Now, unbelievably, we were the owners of a century-old house with apple trees in the garden and an ancient coal hole in the basement. Mac had taken two days off work to help heave furniture into place, and now he'd returned to the office, leaving me to potter around and find homes for all our odds and ends. I waded through the morass of newspapers over the floor, stuck a bucket in the sink and began to fill it with soapy water. I'd fiddled around with the radio and found an oldies station before I started work, and now I sang along with Buddy Holly as I began to wipe the insides of the kitchen cabinets, before loading them with our mugs, plates and pans.

When the doorbell rang I glanced down at myself, in my baggiest, oldest jeans and stained sweatshirt, then went reluctantly to the door. A woman of about my age stood on the doorstep, grinning at me and holding a pie plate.

'Hi, I'm Patty from next door. Just thought I'd stop by with a little something to welcome you to the neighbourhood.' She handed me the pie. 'It's apple.'

'Well, thanks! Would you like to come in? Everything's a mess, of course – including me!'

'Oh, please!' Patty rolled her eyes. 'What do you expect? It's hard work moving into a new house and getting settled.'

I pulled the door open wider. 'I could really do with a break right now, actually. Coffee?' I loved the way women forged friendships so easily here in the Midwest of America.

As the kettle boiled, Patty told me about her kids, ten year old Melissa and six year old Patrick, and her husband Jeff. I stirred the coffee and set it on the table between us.

'I love your house, by the way,' I remarked, taking a seat.

Her grin faded a little. 'Thanks.'

'It's such a beautiful, romantic looking place – you must have a ball decorating it.'

Patty was quiet for a few moments. 'Actually, we're selling up at the end of this year.'

'You're moving?' I was disappointed because I'd taken an immediate liking to her.

'Why?'

'Oh…' Patty shrugged vaguely. 'It's such a cold house.'

'Cold?' I repeated. 'Does your furnace need looking at?'

'It's not that.' She looked uncomfortable. 'The furnace has been checked, and we've had new windows fitted, but nothing has helped. The house is freezing.'

Mystified, I opened my mouth again with another question, but Patty stood abruptly. 'I didn't realize it was so late – the kids will be home from school any minute.'

She left quickly, her coffee almost untouched on the table, and I poured it sadly down the sink. Maybe my comments and questions had been out of line. Obviously she had her reasons for moving, personal ones she couldn't share. Nobody moved because their house was cold.

I decided to take a break from the eternal unpacking the next day and do some work in the garden. It was June now, and fluffy cerise peonies had joined the roses, along with some heavenly blue cornflowers. Bees buzzed industriously from bloom to bloom. I started the mower, shoving it through the luxuriant growth.

Patty's house seemed to loom over me. I glanced over at it a few times, wondering why it always gave off a sense of such quiet, in spite of the fact that it was inhabited by a family of four. The windows were like empty eye sockets. I shivered, turning my back on it as I cut another path through the shaggy grass. When I turned again, someone was watching me from the turret window. A man's thin, pale face regarded me seriously. I began to feel uneasy when his grim gaze didn't waver and he failed to smile. Was this Jeff, I wondered – Patty's husband? I raised my hand and gave a little wave. He moved away from the window, melting into the shadows. Feeling foolish, I lowered my hand. He could at least have waved back.

I told Mac about it that night. He was sitting in bed, yawning as he flipped through the day's paper. I'd just finished brushing my teeth and was massaging a dollop of moisturizer into my face.

'Such a rude man,' I complained.

'Who?' Mac asked.

I sighed. He hadn't been listening; I'd just told him about waving to the man in the window, only to be ignored. 'Patty's husband,' I said. 'Weird looking too.'

I clambered into bed. Normally Mac and I went in for quite a bit of snuggling before we went to sleep but the last few nights had been so hot we'd made do with holding hands while the breeze from the open window cooled us.

'I thought Jeff seemed nice,' Mac said. 'He was taking the trash out as I left for work this morning. Said Hi and everything. Asked how we were settling in.'

'He did?'

'Yup – said to say Hi to you.'

'Didn't you think he looked strange?'

'Strange?' Mac looked at me. 'He just looked like a normal guy. Bit thick around the middle, I guess.'

'I thought he had such intense eyes.' I shuddered, remembering the grim, bony face staring at me unsmilingly this morning.

Mac burst out laughing. 'I'm not sure we're talking about the same guy, Hon. Patty's husband is just your average, friendly guy. Balding, needs to lose a little weight maybe. There was nothing weird, strange or intense about him. He folded his newspaper. 'Now I need to get some sleep.'

I gave him a kiss and switched off the lamp, then lay uneasily in the darkness, listening to the gentle rustle of the trees outside. I could feel the gloomy presence of the house next door, hovering over our back garden. Fear slid through me. Mac had been right – we hadn't been discussing the same man. I had no idea who I'd waved to this morning, but it hadn't been Patty's husband. I lay awake for ages, hoping the knot of fear and tension in my stomach would dissolve, until finally I was lulled by Mac's snores and dozed off.

The next morning I wondered what on earth I could have been so worried about.

It was a bright shiny morning, and I fixed coffee and breakfast before kissing Mac goodbye. In the light of day everything seemed reassuringly normal, and I could have almost chuckled at my silliness of the previous night. I sipped my coffee and glanced outside at the nodding heads of the bright flowers and the pale green mass of the house next door beyond our fruit trees. It was just a rather ornate late-Victorian house, badly in need of a coat of paint. I looked at the windows and they were just windows; no ghostly faces peered out. Maybe I'd imagined what I'd seen yesterday – or maybe I'd disturbed a friend or relative of Patty's with my noisy mowing.

I thought it would be a good idea to get out for a bit. There was a festive atmosphere in town because Cedar Bend was celebrating its centennial. One hundred years ago Cedar Bend had been nothing but a small hamlet with a handful of homes, a general store, church and school. It had prospered over the years, blooming into a small town with a busy High Street, library and its own newspaper.

I headed to the library, my mood as sunny as the weather. I'd been so busy lately with the house, and then so tired by the evening that I hadn't had time to so much as open a book. I planned to remedy that.

The Cedar Bend Library was referred to by locals as the New Building. The old building had burnt to the ground in 1952. A low-slung, sprawling edifice had been designed to replace it, and today it was festooned with bunting flapping gaily in the breeze. An enormous banner hung over the entrance, declaring that Cedar Bend was enjoying its one hundredth birthday.

I browsed around contentedly for over an hour in the large, air conditioned building, pleased to find some recent best sellers. Then I wandered over to a special display of books about the town. Glossy photographs lined an area of wall; plump matrons hosting a town wide potluck in the fifties, an aerial-photograph of the town in 1915, the smouldering remains of the original library after the fire. Then a picture of a house caught my eye and I looked closer, suddenly feeling chilled. It was Patty's house, standing tall and proud on a long ago day when a family called Fischer inhabited it. I looked at the grainy photograph of Abraham Fischer and he gazed back at me implacably, just as he had yesterday as I'd mowed the lawn. His wife sat primly at his side, a plump woman with a nervous expression, and two teenagers, a boy and a girl, hovered behind them.

Waves of dread ran through me as I read the paragraph accompanying the picture. Abraham had been a respected merchant in Cedar Bend at the beginning of the last century. Together he and his wife had run the prosperous general store. Abraham was a quiet, religious man and Mary was a well liked member of the growing community. One summer day, Abraham had left the store early and returned home. His children, Nancy and Thomas, were working in the yard. Their father called them inside and killed the teenagers with blows from his axe – there had been a fearsome struggle, I read, with much resistance. Blood had splashed the walls and floors, smeared the stairs and banisters. Then Abraham had waited for Mary to return home. He had killed her in the hallway, using the axe with which he'd dispatched the children, and then he'd made his way to the top of the house and shot himself cleanly through the head.

I began to shake. My hand came up and covered my mouth. It was so horrible. And it had happened right next door. A friendly library clerk came over. 'Are you okay, ma'am?'

I nodded weakly. 'Just a bit tired.'

She left me as I tried to recover myself. Eventually I left the building, leaving behind my pile of books. All the joy seemed to have drained from the day. Thoughts swirled in my head as I drove home, thoughts of Mary Fischer dying a violent death on a day like this, while flowers bloomed in her garden.

Did Patty know about all this? Was that why she was moving?

Suddenly I wanted to see Patty. I wanted to tell her about the face I'd seen staring at me from the window in her house and not be laughed at, or told I had an over-active imagination.

I parked the car and walked up her path. The neighbourhood lay still and quiet, simmering under the midday heat. I rang Patty's bell and waited. Her front door was broad and wooden, painted dark green. Shuddering, I wondered if it was original. Was this the door Mary Fischer had opened at the end of that day, before her husband met her in the hallway?

217

There was a narrow glass panel at one side of the door and when Patty didn't answer I peered through it. I saw a dim hallway with a narrow table cluttered with mail and the curve of the oak staircase. I imagined bright banners of blood splashing the walls and stairs, and I closed my eyes for a second. Patty wasn't home. I stood back, glancing at my reflection, and then heard the odd rasping sound of my breath as I realized it wasn't my reflection at all. A middle-aged woman peered back at me, her eyes anxious and weary, a shabby bonnet perched on her head. I screamed and flung myself back down the path, my heart thumping wildly.

I wanted to get in the car and drive far, far away, but I had nowhere to go. Instead, I raced into my own house, the house I'd loved so much a few short months ago. I didn't love it anymore – it was too close to something evil.

That night, I told Mac about the picture I'd seen at the library, the information I'd discovered about the house next door. He looked uncomfortable. 'Did you know about this?' I demanded. He'd been raised not twenty minutes from this town.

'I'd heard something, yes,' he admitted. 'There have always been rumours floating around that the house is haunted.'

'And you didn't think to tell me?'

'Tell you what?' He looked irritated as he brushed past me into the kitchen. 'It's not like we live there.'

'I saw something very odd today,' I said as I followed him, my voice trembling. 'I saw Mary

Fischer. Instead of my reflection in Patty's door, I saw hers.'

'You were hot and scared. Your mind played a trick on you, that's all…' he reached to touch me.

I brushed him off. 'I didn't imagine it!'

He shrugged, turning from me to rummage through the fridge and pulling out some cold chicken and salad. 'All that stuff happened a long time ago. Next door is just a house like any other house.'

I stomped angrily out of the kitchen, because I knew that wasn't true. The house next to ours harboured dark, rotten secrets that stuck to its walls like slime.

A few weeks later Patty and Jeff moved without even saying goodbye. It was as if they couldn't wait to be gone. I watched from the window as Patty and the rest of her family climbed into their minivan and drove away. No one looked back.

Summer eased into fall. I had forgiven Mac, although I still wished I'd known about the Fischers when we bought our house. I wasn't particularly superstitious but I believed that some part of that awful day still lingered in the house next door. Dread and unease seemed to ooze from it, pervading everything nearby. I tried to tidy our back garden without looking at the pale green mass beyond our fence, keeping my eyes determinedly on the dead leaves littering our lawn, always returning inside with a feeling of immense relief. I tried to avoid looking at the path Mary Fischer had trudged up, taking her last steps at the end of a long day in the shop, her bonnet slightly askew on her head.

219

What had she been thinking as she opened the door? Had she been wondering what to make for supper moments before Abraham met her with the axe in his hand?

A hundred questions I'd never know the answers to gnawed at me, night and day. What kind of unhappiness had been allowed to fester until it exploded into such horror? All I ever seemed to do was try not to think of it, because if I did, fear spread in me, out of control. In my dreams I ran from Abraham Fischer, up stairs that were slick with blood. The certainty that there was no escape clung, even after I woke up.

One evening Mac returned home just as I was laying supper on the table. He appeared with a big bunch of flowers, a grin on his face. 'I got it,' he said.

My eyes widened. 'The job in Des Moines?' He'd applied a few months ago, not at all sure he'd beat the competition.

Mac nodded happily. 'Can you believe it?'

'Oh, Honey…' My face melted into a big smile.

'We'll have to move,' he said and I nodded, tears of relief rushing into my eyes.

We now live in a very ordinary house that was built in the 1970s, a house that harbours mundane and happy memories of birthday parties and anniversaries. I believe that any secrets this home holds are of a benign nature. Sunshine fills the rather characterless rooms which I'm trying to stamp with personality. We have left Cedar Bend behind. Perhaps one day, I'll be able to forget.

220

A Logical Explanation
By Della Galton

'Mum, this is going to sound ridiculous, but I think Gran's been in the garden.' Mark's eyes are troubled as he looks at me across the dining room table.

I frown. Mark's gran, my mum, died a little over eighteen months ago. Mark adored her. In fact, sometimes I wonder if he's over it, even now.

'What do you mean Lovie?' I keep my voice gentle.

He shifts in his chair. 'Do you remember that time we went to The Chianti for Gran's birthday? You, me, Dad and Gran. The Chianti hadn't been open long so it must have been a good five years ago.'

'It rings a bell – why?'

'Well, we were talking about ghosts and haunting. We were just mucking about, but we got onto the subject of what we'd do if we ever became ghosts. You know, how we'd make our presence felt – just to each other.'

I shake my head. 'I can't say as I remember it.'

'You must do Mum. We all picked something that we do already, to make it easier to remember. I said that if ever I was a ghost, I'd change the

221

channel when you were halfway through watching Coronation Street.'

'Oh yes.' I smile. 'In case there was any proper television on the other side.'

'That's right. And Dad said he'd flick the newspaper open onto the football results.' He hesitates. 'Yours was something to do with curtains, I think.'

'Yes, you're right. I said I'd draw the curtains in the lounge every night because no-one else ever bothers.'

Mark nods. 'Do you remember what Gran said?'

'No, but it must have been something to do with food? She spent all her time in that kitchen. Wasn't it something to do with homemade biscuits?'

'No. Although Dad did suggest that she could leave some on our doorstep, until we decided that a biscuit-making ghost wasn't all that feasible.'

'Housework then?'

'I don't think so.' Mark stands up and goes across to the French windows. He stares out at the garden. 'Although, I think we talked about that too. I seem to remember Gran saying that if ever she got the chance to be a ghost, the last thing she'd want to do was something mundane that she'd done all her life.'

I scrape my chair back and go across to join him. Outside, the evening sunlight slants through the rhododendrons and dapples the grass with gold. I touch Mark's arm and he turns towards me. His eyes are very blue. 'Don't worry Mum,' he says, 'I'm not having a delayed reaction or anything like that.' He hesitates, and looks back into the garden. 'Gran said something else too. She said she loved us all so much that we'd be able to feel her presence without her having to do anything physical. We'd know she hadn't left us.'

'That's right,' I say, but Mark isn't finished.

'I think she changed her mind about that. The *doing something physical* bit I mean.' He unlocks the French windows and steps onto the patio. I follow him outside. One of our neighbours must have cut their grass. The air is full of the scent of it. We go past the fishpond where the lilies have closed their petals for the night, past the shed, overflowing with gardening tools and on towards the bottom of the garden.

'Do you remember how Gran always loved jasmine?' Mark asks, 'But she could never get it to grow because her wall was facing the wrong direction?'

I nod and Mark opens the little gate that leads to the bottom of the garden. We don't come down here much. It's overgrown and weedy and not really in the sun. Right at the end there's an old bench, mildewed and a bit rickety. Jasmine creeps up the wall behind it. In fact, you can hardly see the wall for white flowers. The air is full of their sweet, heady scent.

'It has to be something to do with Gran,' Mark says softly. 'Why else would it be here?'

There's an ache in my throat. I can't bring myself to tell him that his dad planted the jasmine for me earlier this year. Mark obviously hasn't been down here for a while.

223

'I know what you're thinking,' Mark says softly. 'That there has to be some logical explanation.'

'No. I'm not thinking that at all,' I murmur. 'Anyway, you can feel her here, can't you?'

He smiles. His face is sunny, his eyes very peaceful. I decide I'll have to intercept his father before they have a chance to speak. For the first time in my life I wish I didn't have a logical explanation. I wish this really were a message from Mum.

After a while we stroll back inside. 'Fancy a cup of tea, love?' I say, filling up the kettle.

'Please.' Mark picks up the paper from the side. 'Been checking the football results, have you?'

'Certainly not.' I grin as he brandishes the paper.

'Maybe that's Gran too – having a laugh.'

'Maybe.' At least he's smiling. And while I don't think for a minute that the paper being open on the football results has anything to do with Mum, she'd be pleased that he's smiling. Anyway, she was right, we don't need any physical proof to know that she's still around. I still speak to her in my mind every day, I still ask her advice, I can still feel her warmth. I hand Mark his cup of tea and go out into the hallway. The smell of jasmine lingers in the air. It's almost as powerful as when we stood at the bottom of the garden. Perhaps someone has left the lounge windows open, I think, and the wind is in the right direction. It's happened a couple of times before. I open the lounge door. The smell is stronger in here, but I'm halfway across the room before I realise, with a small start of disbelief, that the curtains are already drawn. Behind them, the windows are shut too.

As I stand in the dusk, the scent of jasmine increases in intensity and then fades just as quickly and I'm left with an overwhelming sense of peace. And explanations, logical or otherwise, no longer seem in the least bit important.

The Wheel Of Fortune
By Linda Povey

Angie looked up at the huge construction rising hundreds of feet into the air. It was like an enormous Ferris wheel. But it wasn't at a fairground, it was on the banks of a river.

'Magnificent, isn't it?'

Angie turned to see an older woman, smartly dressed in expensive-looking clothes, smiling at her. Angie had a strange feeling she'd seen her somewhere before. 'Yes, yes, it is,' she replied.

'Are you going to go on it?'

Angie then saw there were glass cubicles attached to the wheel - with people inside them. It was all very scary, like something out of a sci-fi movie.

'Angie, are you getting up? You'll be late for work.'

Angie squinted at the sunlight streaming through the window. She was disappointed her mother's voice had woken her up before the interesting part. For she'd had the dream before.

*   *   *

227

Angie took off the cover of her typewriter and without enthusiasm studied the pile in her in-tray. Her last form teacher at school had told her that the worse thing a girl could do was learn to type, she never got to do anything else. Angie wished she'd listened. She got out a small mirror from her handbag and fiddled with her hair. Mrs. Tyler, the dragon in charge of the typing pool, glared at her.

'Have you got nothing to do, Miss James?' she asked.

'Yes, I've got lots here.' Angie pointed to her in-tray.

'Well, get on with it then.'

Her friend, Marion, at the desk next to hers gave her a sympathetic look, but didn't speak. Chatting in the workplace was an even more heinous crime than preening.

Tony from Purchases, a tall lad with a rather spotty complexion, came over to their table while Angie and Marion were on their tea-break. 'Hi, there,' he said.

'Hi there,' said Marion.

'Hello,' said Angie, raising her eyebrows at Marion. Tony had been trying to get off with her since she'd started work there.

'Angie, fancy coming with us to the Queen's tomorrow night? 'The Inbetweens' are playing.'

'Sorry, can't. Washing my hair,' said Angie.

Tony pulled a face. 'Can't you wash it tonight?'

'No,' said Angie.

Tony shrugged his shoulders, in a see-if-I-care kind of way. 'Please yourself,' he said and strolled off.

Angie sighed. 'Oh, Marion, is this all there is... Grinshill & Sons (Steel Tube & Hollow Sections) Ltd., Mrs. Tyler...and Tony.

'Oh, come on, Angie, it's not so bad. At least you've *got* a job.'

'But it's not what I want. Marion, have you ever fancied working in London? In one of the big offices?'

Marion dipped a biscuit in her tea. 'How's it going to be any different?'

'More opportunities. There's no hope of promotion before you're fifty here. And London's such an exciting place to be.'

'What's brought all this on?'

'Oh, nothing.'

The buzzer sounded to tell them it was time to get back to work.

'No peace for the wicked,' said Marion. 'Come on.'

She had the dream again that night. It was more vivid than ever and this time she wasn't woken up too soon. As before, the woman approached her as she stood gazing up at the big wheel and asked her if she'd like to go on it. Angie wanted to, but she was frightened. The thing was so high.

'It's a wonderful view from up there.'

'Have you been on it?' Angie asked.

'I have,' the woman replied. 'but it's my birthday today, fifty years young, and I'm treating myself to another ride. I'm just off to get my ticket. Would you like me to get you one too?'

Oh what the hell! thought Angie. 'Yes,' she said. 'How much is it?' She inspected her purse. She

229

had a ten-shilling note and some small change on her. She hoped it would be enough.

'Don't worry, I'll treat you.'

The woman disappeared and came back a short while later waving two tickets. 'Come on, lets get in the queue.'

'When will it start to move?' Angie asked. 'Does it go very fast?'

The woman laughed. 'It *is* moving, it's moving all the time. Just very slowly.

It wasn't long before they were way up in the air.

'Where are we?' Angie asked as she gazed at landmarks she thought she recognised nestling amongst tall space-age buildings.

The woman laughed. 'London, of course,' she said. 'There's the Houses of Parliament...that's Tower Bridge...can you make out Nelson's Column in Trafalgar Square? Oh, see that funny-shaped building? The company my husband and I own has its offices there.'

'You own a company?' Angie asked, impressed.

The woman nodded. 'When I was...about your age, I left a dead-end job in a small town to seek my fortune in London. I've never looked back. We've made plans to retire soon, let our son take over the business. We've bought a villa in Spain.'

'That's fantastic,' said Angie.

When they'd gone full circle and reached the ground again, Angie thanked the woman. 'I'm sorry, I never asked your name,' she said.

'It's Angela,' the woman told her.

'Oh,' said Angie, surprised. Same as mine, but they call me Angie.'

The woman smiled. 'They used to call me that too...when I was younger.'

When Angie woke up the next morning, she decided she wasn't going to spend a day longer than she had to at Grinshill & Sons. There was a big wide world out there waiting for her. And she knew where to make a start.

*   *   *

Angie had begun calling herself Angela soon after she came to live in London. She started work as a Junior Clerk in the offices of a small firm of export merchants. She worked her way up to Assistant Manager and when the Managing Director retired, she applied for his job and got it. Through her work, she met her husband, her counterpart in a similar firm. Together they bought the business they now ran.

Angela had often thought about the dream. In many ways, she'd become the woman she'd shared the ride with. She and her husband had even talked of retiring early and going to live in Spain, leaving the company in their son's hands.

But it was easy to analyse. A case of wish-fulfilment, she reasoned. The woman was her future self, as her subconscious wished her to be. She'd simply set out to make her a reality. As for the wheel, that represented life's 'wheel of fortune', which her fertile imagination had conjured up. It was all quite rational.

Then they'd started building the London Eye.

*   *   *

It's the night of her fiftieth birthday. Angela is dreaming. She's made her way to the Eye and is scouring the area, in search of the teenage girl she'd once been. It's a weird feeling when she finds her. The girl is staring up at the wheel.

Angela walks up to her. 'Magnificent, isn't it?' she says with a smile.

Animal Magic
By Jill Steeples

I swear to God, if ever a masked madman intent on all things dastardly were to enter our house in the middle of the night, Rick would happily snooze his way through the whole darn thing. As it was, I was sitting bolt upright in bed, stricken with terror, not wanting to contemplate who or what was making the heavy thumping noises coming from downstairs.

'Rick,' I hissed, elbowing his sleeping lump in the ribs. 'Did you hear that?'

'Uhh,' he grunted, furrowing further beneath the duvet like a piglet.

'That noise,' I whispered in his ear, 'I think there's someone in the house.'

'Okay, love, I'll sort it in the morning,' he mumbled heroically, snuggling deeper into the ten tog.

So much for my knight in shining armour, I thought wryly. As if I had any chance of sleeping, with Ivan the Terrible lurking around downstairs. Sensibly, I should have hidden under the covers and pulled a pillow over my head, but for some reason, I felt a strange compulsion to venture into the darkness. Throwing on a T-shirt, I slipped my feet into my mules and grabbed the copy of 'Homely

Homes' lying on my bedside table, rolling it up in my fist.

The first night in your new home should be a night to remember, but I was beginning to think it might be remembered for all the wrong reasons. 'Newlywed found bludgeoned in countryside idyll,' the headline would read. Rick would be a broken man, living the remainder of his years, guilt-ridden and lovelorn, mourning his beautiful young wife, who'd met a tragic end one autumn night.

A cold shiver whipped through my body and goose bumps stood proudly on my arms as I tiptoed stealthily along the unfamiliar landing. A picture of Jack Nicholson's maniacal face appearing from behind a doorway popped into my head and the thought made me giggle and shudder at the same time. I crept down the wooden staircase, negotiating the piles of boxes in the hallway, taking time to peer into each of the rooms. There was nothing, only the curious emptiness of unloved, neglected rooms and a faint whiff of the countryside. But then we were in the country, I reminded myself and after years of living in the hubbub of the city, the eerie quietness might take some getting used to.

The wind howled outside causing the side gates to fling open and bang noisily against the orchard wall. My heart leapt at the sound. I peered through the window and caught glimpses of shadows flickering on the brickwork in the half-light. I tried to steady my breathing. That's all it was, I told myself. Not a mass murderer lying in wait, just a gate banging in the wind. I hurried back up the stairs, jumped into bed and placed my icy feet against Rick's warm sleeping body, unable to rid myself of the thought that we'd inherited house-guests in the move.

Things would seem better in the morning, I told myself, but over breakfast the next day, I couldn't shake off the cloak of unease that had wrapped itself around my shoulders, ever since we'd taken possession of the keys.

'Lizzie, you've got an over-active imagination, that's your trouble,' Rick said, dismissively. 'Anyway, you haven't got time to worry about fanciful night-time visitors. That skip needs filling by lunch, so you'd better get a move on.' He gave me a friendly slap on the bottom as I made my way into the kitchen, while he took a sledgehammer to a party wall.

It had been love at first sight when Rick first spotted the house. He'd come home bubbling with enthusiasm for the rundown Victorian villa, that he'd discovered tucked away down a country lane, euphemistically described by the agent as having potential. I didn't share his vision, couldn't imagine how we could turn the crumbling decaying shell into our dream home, but Rick was determined not to let the opportunity pass. He got to work drawing up plans, sketching a light and airy open-plan living space that was unrecognisable from the existing dark and dingy rooms.

'And, of course,' he'd said, showing me the ramshackle barn at the bottom of the garden, 'that outbuilding would make an ideal studio for you.' It was an inspired move by Rick. He knew it was my dream to have my own garden studio, somewhere to sit and design the greetings cards that made up my fledgling business. Eager not to miss out, we quickly signed up for the house in the country.

Now, as I deposited the contents of the wheelbarrow into the skip, I wondered if we might come to regret our decision. Stretched to the limit of our budget, we'd have to do all the work ourselves and even though Rick's the practical type, I couldn't help wondering if we'd taken on more than we could manage. As if reading my thoughts, a voice called out from behind me.

'You've a job on there.' The good-natured rustic burr belonged to a stout, red-cheeked gentleman. 'Bob,' he said, holding out his hand, by way of introduction. 'Wingbury born and bred, so anything you need to know, I'm your man.'

But there wasn't anything I needed to ask because Bob proceeded to tell me everything he knew about the village and our house.

'This was a butcher's shop at one time, you know,' he started.

'Really,' I said, feeling my spine tingle at his words, but why, I couldn't be sure. I beckoned to Rick to come and join us.

'Oh, yes,' said Bob, eager to impart his news, 'let me show you. This old front door here was the entrance to the house and round here was the opening to the shop.' He walked round to the side gate, to show us the bricked up doorway. 'And that up there,' he said, with what I considered an unnecessary amount of glee, 'was the slaughterhouse.' He was pointing at the dilapidated barn, what was to be my studio.

My stomach flipped in disgust.

'I can clearly remember seeing the cows being led down the High Street,' he continued, 'through the lane and up the driveway into the abattoir for …'

Umm nice, I thought, wishing my garden hideaway could have hidden a more romantic past! I didn't want to hear the gory details.

'Fascinating,' I said, cutting Bob off in mid-sentence. But Bob's tales, as we came to discover, were fascinating. It transpired that the house next door had been the bakers shop, although somewhat disappointingly, I never did find out if there had been a candlestick maker. Our sleepy back road had once been the centre of the village.

Later that day Rick called me up into the bedroom.

'Seems that Bob's right,' he said. 'Take a look at these.' He had the floorboards up and was pointing at some metal brackets positioned over the joists.

'What are they?'

'They've been cut off, but they were obviously hooks down into the front room for the joints of meat to hang on.'

I'd imagined living in the home of a famous author, a poet or countrywoman, picking up on the creative vibes left wafting in the atmosphere. But a butcher's shop had never figured on my wish-list. It was something to do with all those animals, the blood and the gore; it left a nasty aftertaste in my mouth. Rick, of course, thought I was utterly mad.

'This house and its quirky history is our home now. Stop spooking yourself and make the most of it.'

237

In the nights that followed, we fell into bed, exhausted after our physical efforts, and every night, without fail, I was woken by the strange midnight callings that had accompanied our arrival. I lay in bed listening to the creepy creaking of the wooden gates and the soulful animal noises that pervaded the air. Rick was dead to the world, caught up in his dreams of DIY, but I lay awake trying to make sense of those night-time sounds.

Over the next months the house slowly took shape. New wooden sash windows were installed, original slate flooring laid in the kitchen and oak floorboards fitted in the rest of the downstairs rooms. Walls were knocked through to make an airy open living area that was modern, yet still retained much of its original charm.

Some months later, Bob, who by now had become a regular visitor, turned up early one evening laden down with trays of brightly coloured Michaelmas daisies.

'Thought these might look good in that old sink of yours.'

'What a lovely idea, Bob.' I said, taking them from him. The old butler sink had been dismantled from the outhouse, given a thorough cleaning and with Bob's flowers would make a welcoming feature for the front of the studio. In the space of a year, we'd fulfilled our dream, managing to turn the crumbling house into an enviable home and the outbuilding into a practical design studio.

'Do you know what Lizzie thinks about this place?' said Rick, coming out to join us with a celebratory bottle of wine and three glasses.

'What's that then?' asked Bob.

'That the place is haunted.' Rick laughed, unable to hide his scepticism. 'But not by any old ghost, you understand, but by the ghosts of all the animals that came through those gates.'

'It's true,' I said, blushing under Bob's direct gaze. 'I felt it as soon as we moved in, a strange lingering presence in the property.' I thought back to that first night and my run-in with my imagined monster. Had it been just my imagination, I wondered, or a welcoming offering?

'Well, if you want to hear ghost stories about this place,' Bob said, his eyes lighting up at the chance, 'I can tell you a tale or two that will raise the hackles on your back.'

'Er, no, I don't think so, thank you, Bob,' I said, smiling. It didn't matter any more. I'd grown used to our new home and all its strange noises, finding them comforting rather than disturbing. I put a friendly arm around Bob's shoulder. 'Instead, why don't we raise a toast to our new home, to you Bob for all your help and encouragement, and to the new business premises of Daisy Designs.'

'Daisy Designs!' said Bob and Rick raising their glasses in unison, laughing.

And later that night, as I lay in bed listening to our creaking side gates swaying in the wind, I like to think I could hear the animals singing under the moonlit sky.

Elysium
By Andrea Presneill

e-liz(h)i-am, (n) among the Greeks, the abode of
the blessed dead (myth) any delightful place

My mother was born with psychic powers so her
predictions were part of everyday life and I grew up
believing in ghosts and spirits. Not so my son.
'Bunkum,' he'd laugh. 'There's no such thing.
Ghosts are the product of an over-active
imagination, or it's a trick of the light, or there's a
reasonable explanation.'

Then a strange event changed his mind.

At the time, Craig and his partner Louise were
students. They were broke but decided they needed a
holiday anyway. As luck would have it, they found a
cheap flight to Tunisia, and backpacked the country
for a week. Then it was on to mainland Greece,
which was disappointingly noisy, crowded and
commercialised. So, after a day or two, they took a
ferry to the islands.

Paros, at the time was, and may still be, trendy
and touristy with a long strip of rowdy nightclubs
and bars. Still not the 'real' Greece they had hoped
for. So they decided to try Antiparos, which, they
were assured, was very tiny and very quiet—far
more their scene.

The day they arrived was hot, humid, with a sun-filled sky and a few clouds that hung like cannon puffs of smoke. Delighted with what they saw, they opted to stay for the few remaining days of their holiday and went into a shop to ask if anyone could recommend a room to rent.

'Ah, you have come to the right place,' the man said. 'Come, follow me and I show you.'

Upstairs was a large two-bedroom apartment, partly used for storage, with pots and pans which still had price stickers on. Craig and Louise loved the place but knew it would be outside their price range, and reluctantly said so. But to their amazement, they were offered it at a pittance. The pair could hardly believe their luck and assumed it must be owned by a holiday company but was not yet decorated for rental purposes, and in the meantime the shop was cashing in on the side.

'Good for them,' was their attitude.

After settling in, they decided to find somewhere to eat. The road to town was hard-packed mud, topped with a fine white powder that spun up in a cloud as they walked. Bushes and shrubs were dwarfed and dusty, sometimes strewn with thimble-sized ruby flowers. The few random houses cast blunt shadows, and no-one was about.

The tiny town consisted of three main streets—one that led back to their flat, and two that branched off. Along each were a few small enterprises, mostly cafes, tavernas and gift shops. There were also a few derelict boarded-up buildings that, presumably, had once been shops too.

After exploring, the pair decided to have a drink before dinner. They returned to the original street and, set in a row of shops, they came across a small, plain, almost stark building. Clearly this was no tourist attraction. There were no tables and chairs outside, no swinging sign, no name above the door. Intrigued, Craig cupped a hand and peered through the window to see an old-fashioned taverna, two customers and a barman pouring drinks.

Delighted at this authentic slice of the real Greece, they went inside. It was dim after the piercing sunlight, cool, lit with a few candles and old lamps. The wooden benches and tables were long and pockedmarked with usage, as was the bare wooden floor, and although everywhere was clean enough there was still a sense of dusty agelessness about the place that was pleasing and atmospheric.

At a corner table two elderly men looked up from a backgammon board and nodded a welcome. Good natured and polite banter was exchanged by all, with much gesturing and smiling, neither side able to understand the other. It was perhaps unusual that the Greeks didn't speak a word of English, but this was a tiny island, and it added to the old-world charm.

After a while, the men hunched over their board again and Craig went to the bar to order. He noticed there were no optics or spirits, no brand-name bottles. Nor were there any beer or lager pumps, and no cans of any kind, not even the ubiquitous Coke, Pepsi, or 7 Up, let alone beer. All drinks were in thick, unlabelled, old-fashioned glass-stoppered bottles.

Craig mimed and pointed while repeating, 'Two ouzos with ice, please,' and after discussion with the elderly men, the barman took up an old flip-top flagon and poured the drinks. Water was added from an ancient, dimpled metal jug. Ice, apparently, was not available.

As he and Louise slid onto a wooden bench, the barman arrived with a plate of olives, bread and a variety of fish and cheese. Thanking him, Craig tried to pay, but the barman shook his head and waved his hands in negation.

It was very quiet. The old men played backgammon in silence, the barman watched. There was no piped music, no clocks or calendars. Not a coaster or napkin anywhere and no cutlery. There wasn't even a cigarette machine in sight. It was as if time had frozen. Like a stage play, the Greeks wore collarless open-necked shirts, sleeves rolled above the elbows. Their trousers were thick, their boots heavy. None wore watches, rings or jewellery of any kind.

As soon as glasses emptied, more ouzo and food was produced. Craig and Louise commented on how totally relaxed and happy they felt in this gentle, unspoilt atmosphere. Contentedly, they looked out the window. A number of tourists and locals sauntered by but no one came into the taverna.

'Don't know what they're missing,' Craig remarked.

'Yes, but have you noticed that not one person has so much as glanced in here,' Louise commented idly. It was perhaps odd, but they thought no more about it.

Time passed. Both said they had never felt happier; it was as if they were cocooned in a bubble of peace and tranquillity. The only drawback was that they'd had a number of rounds of ouzo and plates of food, but the barman could not be persuaded to accept payment no matter how hard they pressed. Eventually, Craig and Louise were unsure what to do. They wanted to stay and make a night of it, but only if they could pay their way. True, they were poor students, but shrank from the notion of being seen as English spongers, especially as the taverna clearly wasn't a prosperous and thriving concern. And so, very reluctantly, after profuse thanks and prolonged and courteous goodbyes from the barman and customers, the pair left.

As they made their way back to the flat they agreed they wanted to spend their remaining evenings in the taverna.

'There's a way round it,' Craig remarked. 'We can go back tomorrow night and buy everyone several rounds of drinks; then we'll leave the money and a big tip on the table and race out the door if we have to.'

Next day they went to town but didn't find the taverna. No matter. A number of shops shut for the afternoon anyway and they had probably past it without realising. Hours drifted by as they explored the town, bought a few souvenirs and postcards and had a leisurely lunch.

By evening, they decided it was time for a drink and they made their way back to the taverna. But there was no sign of it. They went up and down the row of shops several times but still no taverna. Both were sure this was the right street as it was the only one that lead directly back to the flat. But after searching again, they eventually decided they must be mistaken. So saying, they checked the town and the other two streets but found nothing remotely resembling their taverna. Finally, they went back to the original spot, convinced that this was the right place. But there was nothing there except a small derelict building boarded up with weather-beaten planks and rusted nails.

Bewildered now, they asked a number of locals about the taverna, but were met with polite shrugs of indifference. No one knew of such a place in this location. This building had been boarded up for as long as anyone could remember. Some asked for the name of the taverna, which, of course, the pair couldn't supply. More shrugs—they must be mistaken. Perhaps the taverna was on another street. It seemed no one wanted to discuss the matter, or they simply weren't interested. It was hard to tell which. In England the story would have provoked much interest, a topic to be mulled over, discussed; explanations put forward. But not here.

However, after persevering for some time, an elderly Greek told them there had been a taverna once, and on the very spot, but that was a long time ago and it had been boarded up for many years. He couldn't or wouldn't shed any light on the matter. Like the others, he was indifferent. They were mistaken and that was the end of it.

In the end, Craig and Louise gave up and got on with enjoying the rest of their holiday. Even so, every time they went to town they checked on the taverna, but it was always boarded up.

Sadly, it remained a small mystery that was never solved, but my son and his wife now believe in spirits and time-slips.

Biographies

Kathryn Brennan, having always gained particular enjoyment from writing, became a full-time writer in January 2004. She has had work published in Muso magazine and is currently working on a novel.

Tina Brown lives two hours south of Sydney, Australia. Her writing has won a number of prizes in competitions including one by Mills and Boon. Tina is a veteran of the 'Shorts' range as her stories featured in 'Sexy Shorts for Christmas' and 'Sexy Shorts For Summer'

Anne Caulfield is a professional medium. In 1999 she was advised to write about the psychic side of her life. Ann has written short stories for competitions and had a mini saga published in the Daily Telegraph. Her book Pathway To Spirit published by Zambezi is available from September 2004.

Kathleen Croft was born and grew up in Yorkshire. Now widowed she is retired and has four grown up children. She has recently completed a MA in Creative Writing at Lancaster University. Kathleen had a story published in 'Sexy Shorts for Summer'.

Elizabeth Crooks and her husband now live in Shropshire after many years of moving around England, Singapore and Germany with the armed forces. She has recently decided to fulfil a life-long ambition to write, having completed a novel length account of her years as the wife of a serviceman, and had many short stories published. Elizabeth is now half-way through a murder mystery.

Sasha Fenton worked as a professional astrologer, palmist and Tarot card reader for over twenty years. She has written star-sign columns for a number of magazines and newspapers, lectures all over the world, served on a number of committees and guilds and appeared on many TV and radio programmes. Her books have sold over six million copies worldwide. She, together with her husband, runs Zambezi Publishing.

Yvette Fielding first appeared on TV aged thirteen and in June 1987 she became Blue Peter's youngest presenter. Yvette went on to present many TV shows. She and her cameraman/producer husband founded Antix Productions which is responsible for 'Most Haunted', Living TV's show Yvette lives in the UK with her husband and two children.

Della Galton has had over 500 stories and features published by women's magazines and also writes serials and features. She has three novels awaiting publication and contributed to Sexy Shorts for Summer. Della lives by the sea with her husband and four dogs.

Liza Granville has an MA in Creative Writing from the University of Plymouth and is currently researching for a PhD. A considerable number of her short stories have been published in magazines and on the web. A collection 'Baiting The Unicorn' was published by Bastard Books and her novel 'Curing A Pig' is published by Flame Books.

Hilary Halliwell lives in Dorset with her partner and two rescue cats. She writes short stories and articles for a number of popular women's magazines. Hilary has just completed her first children's novel and two series of storybooks. She is presently plotting her first mainstream fiction novel.

Jim Harwood started writing earnestly in 1988 after moving to Pembrokeshire to raise a family. He spent five years as a performance poet, publishing two anthologies and recording for TV and radio. He has now retired and continues to challenge accepted artistic conventions wherever they be.

Raymond Humphreys was born in London and has lived in Wales since 1972. Formerly a local government officer, he now writes and reviews regularly for a number of publications. His work has been published all over the world as well as on the internet.

Jan Jones featured in 'Sexy Shorts for Summer' and has had short stories published in a variety of women's magazines. She is currently working on a contemporary romantic comedy novel.

Carolyn Lewis recently graduated from the University of Glamorgan with an MPhil in writing. Her work has been printed in a variety of publications and her short stories in a number of anthologies. Carolyn is presently working on her second novel whilst tutoring part-time in Creative Writing.

Lisa Main lives in Bath with her husband, two children and Dalmatian puppy, Mac. She has had stories published in several magazines and was runner up in Woman writing competition 2001. Lisa has recently submitted her first novel, 'Keeping the Faith' to the Romantic Novelist Association.

Sue Moorcroft writes short fiction and serials for magazines in several countries. She has won or been runner-up in a number of national competitions. Sue is a member of the Romantic Novelist Association and featured in 'Sexy Shorts for Christmas'.

Sandy Neville has written many short stories and is currently working on her first children's novel. She has had great success in competitions, most notably Sandy was a finalist in Channel 4's, Richard and Judy 'Write a Children's Story' competition.

David Peck is a self-employed writer and researcher. He has published a number of articles and a book about careers education and guidance. David is a student of Creative Writing in Shrewsbury, his other interests include walking and wildlife watching.

Linda Povey's first success came with the publication of verses for greeting cards, she now writes short stories for popular women's magazines. Linda has recently become involved in running residential courses for short story writers. She is a part-time teacher in Shropshire.

Andrea Presneill lives in Bristol and has five grown-up sons and seven grandchildren. She was recently short-listed for the Romantic Novelists Association RD Award. Andrea writes full-time and has had a Romantic Suspense novel published as well as a story in 'Sexy Shorts for Summer'.

Jillian Rawlins has written numerous theatrical interpretations for National Parks and Theatre in Education programmes on a wide range of topics. Jillian lives in Pembrokeshire with her co-author husband and four golden retrievers.

Patricia Scott has won four awards for her writing. Her main writing interests are romantic historicals and crime novels. She is a retired Army wife with four children.

Jill Steeples lives in Leighton Buzzard with her husband and two children. She is a published writer and enjoys creating short stories for the popular women's magazines. Jill is an enthusiastic member of both her local writers' circle and an internet based writers group.

Jill Stitson had her first story published at age twelve and has had an interest in writing ever since. Since retiring she has joined a Creative Writing class and was recently a prize winner in the Writers News magazine short story competition.

Peter Stockwell is an architect who has written from an early age. He has had work published in a number of magazines and anthologies. Peter also collaborates with his wife, children's author Robyn Dalby-Stockwell, in writing stories and poetry. He is presently working on a novel.

Nina Tucknott has written hundreds of articles and short stories for magazines and anthologies. She is presently working on her first novel. Nina is a Swedish speaking Finn who now lives in Brighton with her husband and teenage sons.

Jay Whitfield lives in Carmarthenshire with her husband, dog and numerous pet sheep. She has been writing for five years and has had short stories and articles published in writers' magazines. Her collection of short stories, 'Love Bites' was published on the internet and a historical epic about ghosts is in the pipeline.

Angela Williams, originally from Hereford, now lives in Holland with her husband. She added to her degree in Textiles with a writing course via the Open College of the Arts and Ty Newydd. She writes fiction and poetry.

Dawn Wingfield was born in London and now lives in Colorado USA with her husband and four children. Several of Dawn's stories have appeared online and in small press magazines and she is presently working on her first novel.

A Message From
Breast Cancer Campaign

The Facts About Breast Cancer

Breast cancer is the commonest form of cancer in the UK, with one woman in nine developing breast cancer.

Each year over 40,000 women are newly diagnosed with breast cancer and on average 12,840 women will die from the disease.

Men can also suffer from breast cancer and about 90 men die from the disease a year.

In the UK breast cancer is the second biggest cause of death from cancer in women.

Breast Cancer Campaign believes that research is the only way forward if we are to prevent so many people dying from this disease.

The Difference We Make Through Your Support

Breast Cancer Campaign is the only charity that specialises in funding independent research into breast cancer throughout the UK. The Charity is currently funding fifty research projects, worth over £5.6 million, in sixteen cities across the UK.

Breast Cancer Campaign aims to find the cure for breast cancer by funding research which looks at improving diagnosis and treatment of breast cancer, better understanding how it develops and ultimately either curing the disease or preventing it.

In the same way that breast cancer is not one disease, there will not be one cure. Breast Cancer Campaign's jigsaw piece logo symbolises the missing pieces of the puzzle that is the cure for breast cancer. Each research project is another piece of the puzzle that we hope will offer women with breast cancer effective diagnosis and treatment and eventually help us prevent the disease.

**To find out more about the work we do visit us at
www.breastcancercampaign.org**

How to be Breast Aware

Be Breast Aware - The best way to influence your chance of surviving breast cancer is to detect it early, so be breast aware and know what is normal for you, then you can act if you notice something wrong.

Look for these changes, and remember, if you are in any doubt visit your doctor.

...Look

Look at yourself in the mirror, look for changes that are unusual. For example:

Any change in the shape or size of the breast or nipple.

Any change in the position or colouring of the nipple, including inversion.

Any dimpling, denting, scaling or discolouration of the skin.

...Feel

Feel your breasts, feel for anything that is not normally there. For example:

A lump or swelling in your breast, that feels different from the rest of your breast tissue.

A lump or swelling in the armpit, arm or around your collarbone.

...Be Breast Aware

Recognise any other changes. For example:

Discharge from one or both nipples.

A pain in the breast, armpit or arm that is new for you.

259

Report any changes that you find to your doctor without delay, and if you are aged fifty or over, attend routine breast screening.

Guardian Angel

It can be difficult to remember to check your breasts, so why not let Guardian Angel help you with her diary sticker bookmark. The bookmark features twelve small stickers to be stuck in your diary on the same day each month as a subtle reminder, and also highlights the changes to look out for.

Guardian Angel is the Charity's breast awareness ambassador and aims to make people more breast aware.

To order your bookmark please call Breast Cancer Campaign on 020 7749 3700

We need your help and your support.

Research into the causes, early diagnosis, specific treatment and the eventual prevention of this terrible disease is vital in helping to save lives.
Please help us to continue with our vital research work.

Yes, I want to help in the fight against breast cancer.

Please accept my donation of £.....................
Or
Debit my credit/CAF Card no:

| | | | | | | | | | | | | | | | | | |

Expiry date.................... Amount £...................

Signature ....

Name...

Address...

....

....Postcode...........................

Gift Aid declaration

To make your money go further sign here

....

This will increase the value of your donation by almost a third at no extra cost to you! If you are a UK tax payer, BCC will be able to reclaim tax on your donation.

Please send this page to:
Breast Cancer Campaign
Clifton Centre
110 Clifton Street
London EC2A 4HT
Tel: 020 7749 3700 Fax: 020 7749 3701
www.breastcancercampaign.org

Registered Charity number 299758

261

the Dungeons

A unique combination of real history, horror and humour bring gruesome goings-on back to life in the 21st century. The Dungeons invite you to a unique feast of fun with history's horrible bits. Live actors, rides shows and special effects transport you back to those bleak, black times.

Are you brave enough?

www.thedungeons.com